MARY DOWNING HAHN

took

a ghost story graphic novel

Adapted by
Scott Peterson,
Jen Vaughn,
and ## Hank Jones

Etch
Clarion Books
Imprints of HarperCollins*Publishers*
Boston   New York

For Pete, Joan, and Devin for giving me the chance to work on such a cool project.
And for Jen for doing such a great job on the art.
And, as always, here's to Story.
—Scott Peterson

To Kyla Gay for the love, Pete Friedrich for the guidance,
my coworking buds for the support, and all the shadows for the company
—Jen Vaughn

Etch and Clarion Books are imprints of HarperCollins Publishers.

Took
Copyright © 2022 by HarperCollins Publishers LLC
Adapted from *Took* by Mary Downing Hahn
Copyright © 2015 by Mary Downing Hahn

Library of Congress Cataloging-in-Publication Data has been applied for.
ISBN: 978-0-358-53688-8 hardcover
ISBN: 978-0-358-53687-1 paperback

Colorist: Hank Jones
Lettering by Morgan Martinez
Flatters: Frank Reynoso, Laura Martin, and Christiana Tushaj
The illustrations in this book were done in Clip Studio Paint on an iPad.
The text was set in Ashcan, Nightwatcher, and Evil Doings.
Cover design by Catherine San Juan and Pete Friedrich
Interior design by Pete Friedrich

Manufactured in Canada
Friesens 10 9 8 7 6 5 4 3 2 1
45XXXXXXXX

First Edition

took

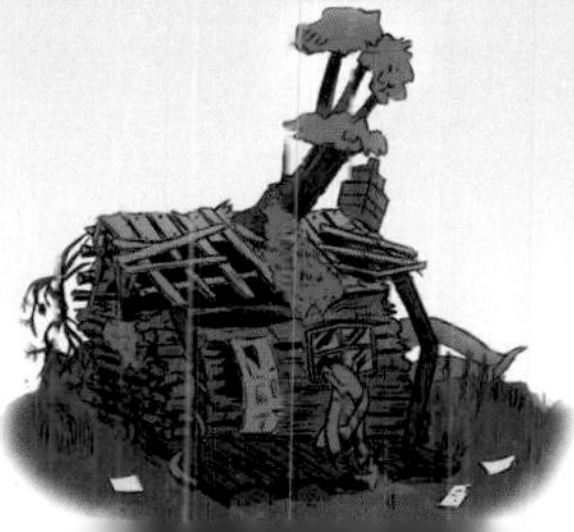

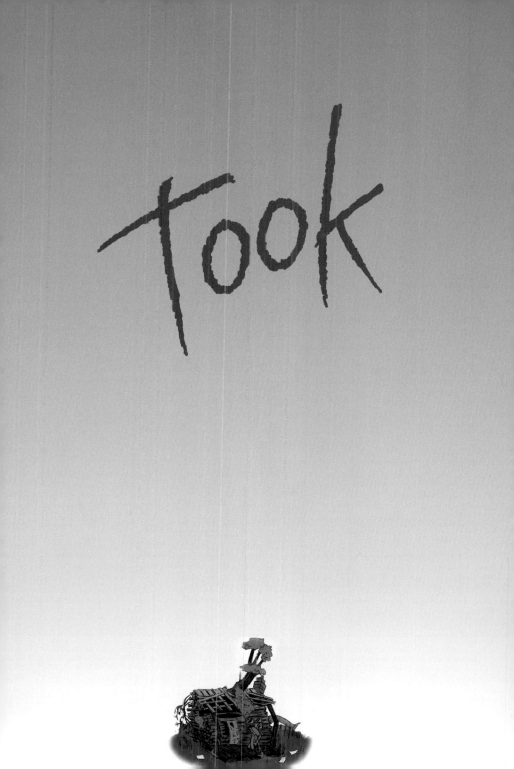

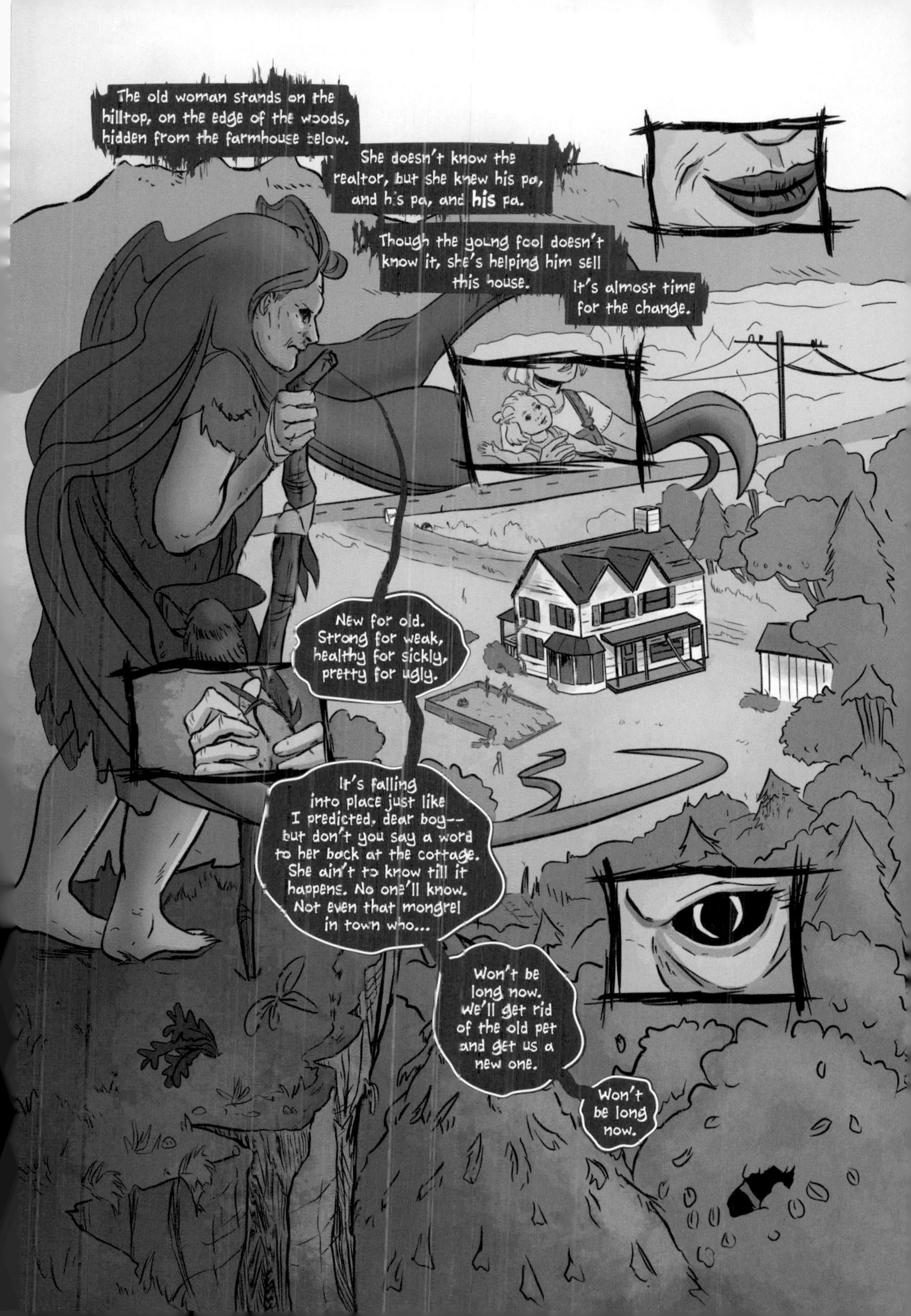
The old woman stands on the hilltop, on the edge of the woods, hidden from the farmhouse below.
She doesn't know the realtor, but she knew his pa, and his pa, and **his** pa.
Though the young fool doesn't know it, she's helping him sell this house.
It's almost time for the change.
New for old. Strong for weak, healthy for sickly, pretty for ugly.
It's falling into place just like I predicted, dear boy--but don't you say a word to her back at the cottage. She ain't to know till it happens. No one'll know. Not even that mongrel in town who...
Won't be long now. We'll get rid of the old pet and get us a new one.
Won't be long now.

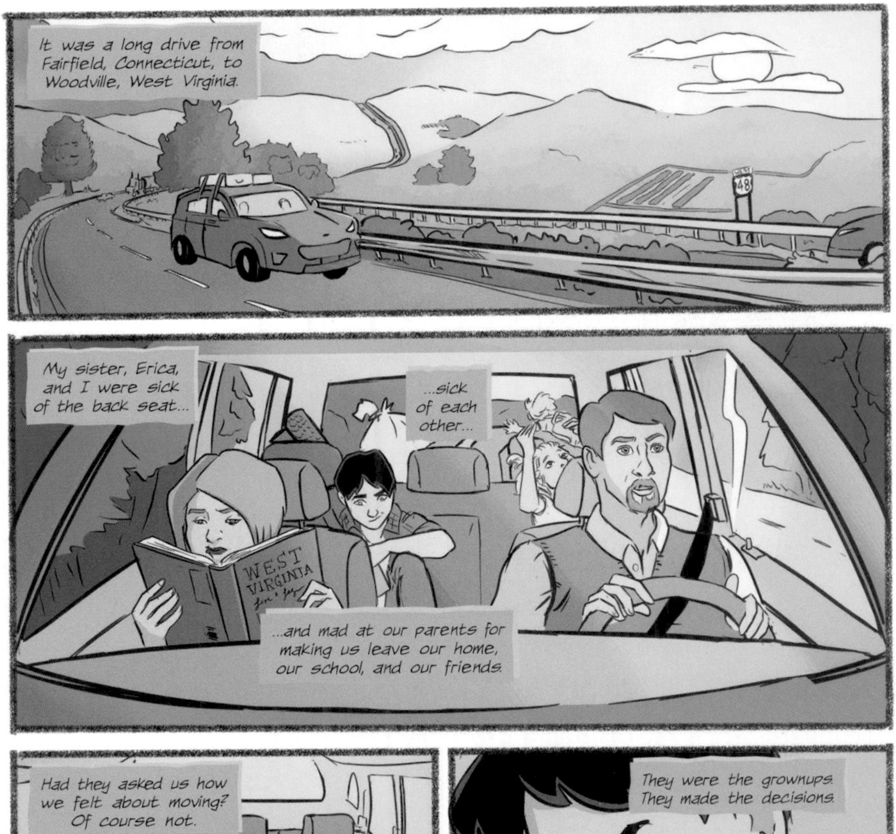
It was a long drive from Fairfield, Connecticut, to Woodville, West Virginia.
My sister, Erica, and I were sick of the back seat...
...sick of each other...
WEST VIRGINIA
...and mad at our parents for making us leave our home, our school, and our friends.
Had they asked us how we felt about moving? Of course not.
They'd left us with a neighbor, driven down, found a house, and bought it. Just like that.
They were the grownups. They made the decisions.
They had a reason.
Dad worked for a big corporation.
He earned a big salary. We had a big house, two big cars.
Erica and I went to private school.
Mom drove me and Erica and our friends to games and team practice and the country club.

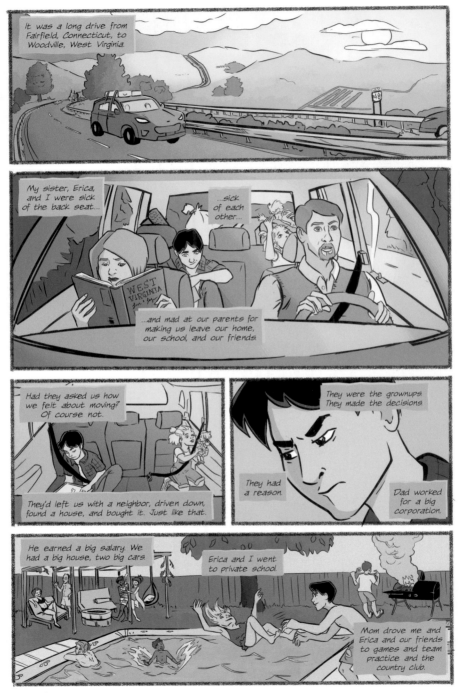

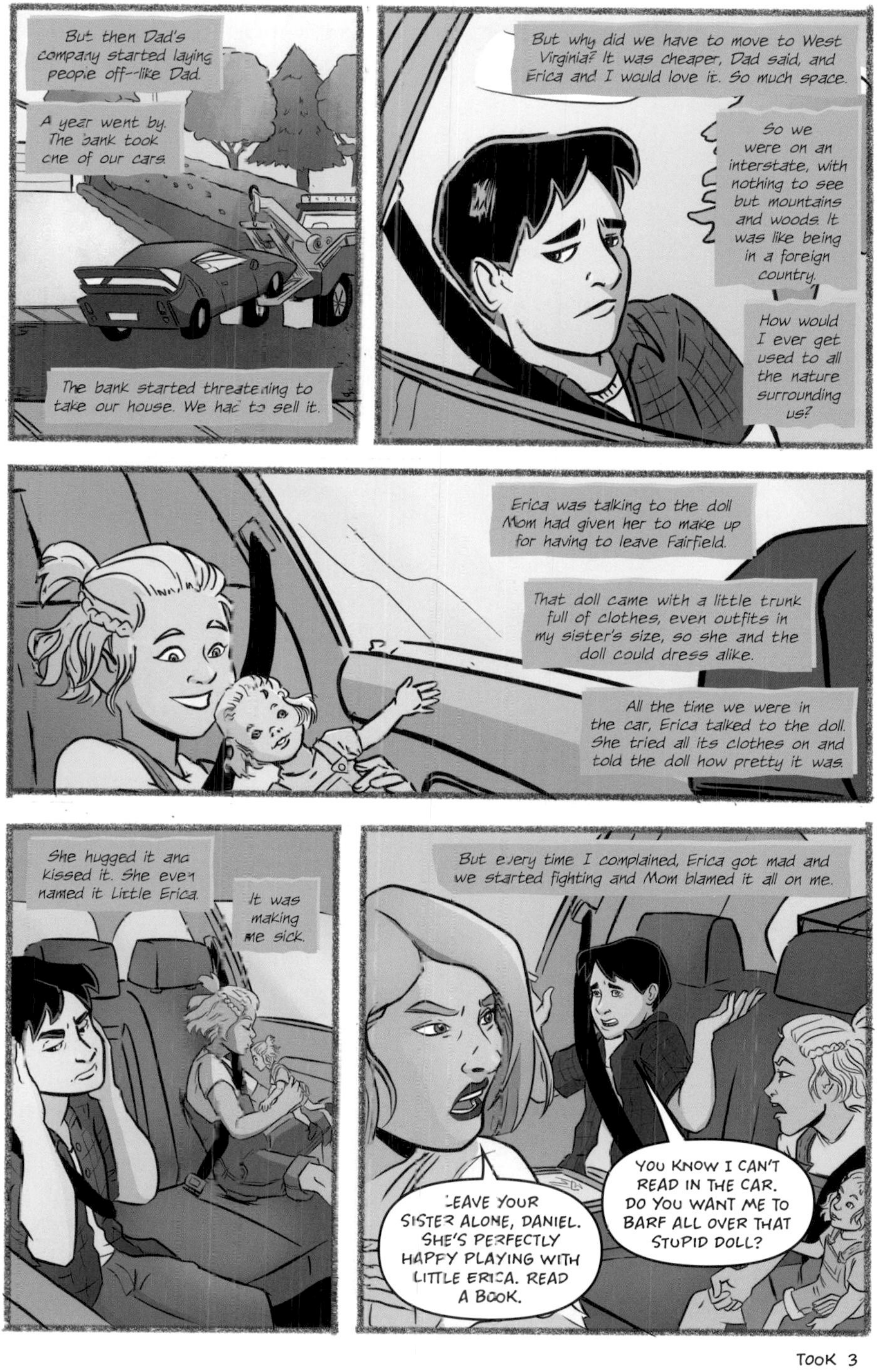
But then Dad's company started laying people off--like Dad.
A year went by. The bank took one of our cars.
The bank started threatening to take our house. We had to sell it.
But why did we have to move to West Virginia? It was cheaper, Dad said, and Erica and I would love it. So much space.
So we were on an interstate, with nothing to see but mountains and woods. It was like being in a foreign country.
How would I ever get used to all the nature surrounding us?
Erica was talking to the doll Mom had given her to make up for having to leave Fairfield.
That doll came with a little trunk full of clothes, even outfits in my sister's size, so she and the doll could dress alike.
All the time we were in the car, Erica talked to the doll. She tried all its clothes on and told the doll how pretty it was.
She hugged it and kissed it. She even named it Little Erica.
It was making me sick.
But every time I complained, Erica got mad and we started fighting and Mom blamed it all on me.
YOU KNOW I CAN'T READ IN THE CAR. DO YOU WANT ME TO BARF ALL OVER THAT STUPID DOLL?
LEAVE YOUR SISTER ALONE, DANIEL. SHE'S PERFECTLY HAPPY PLAYING WITH LITTLE ERICA. READ A BOOK.

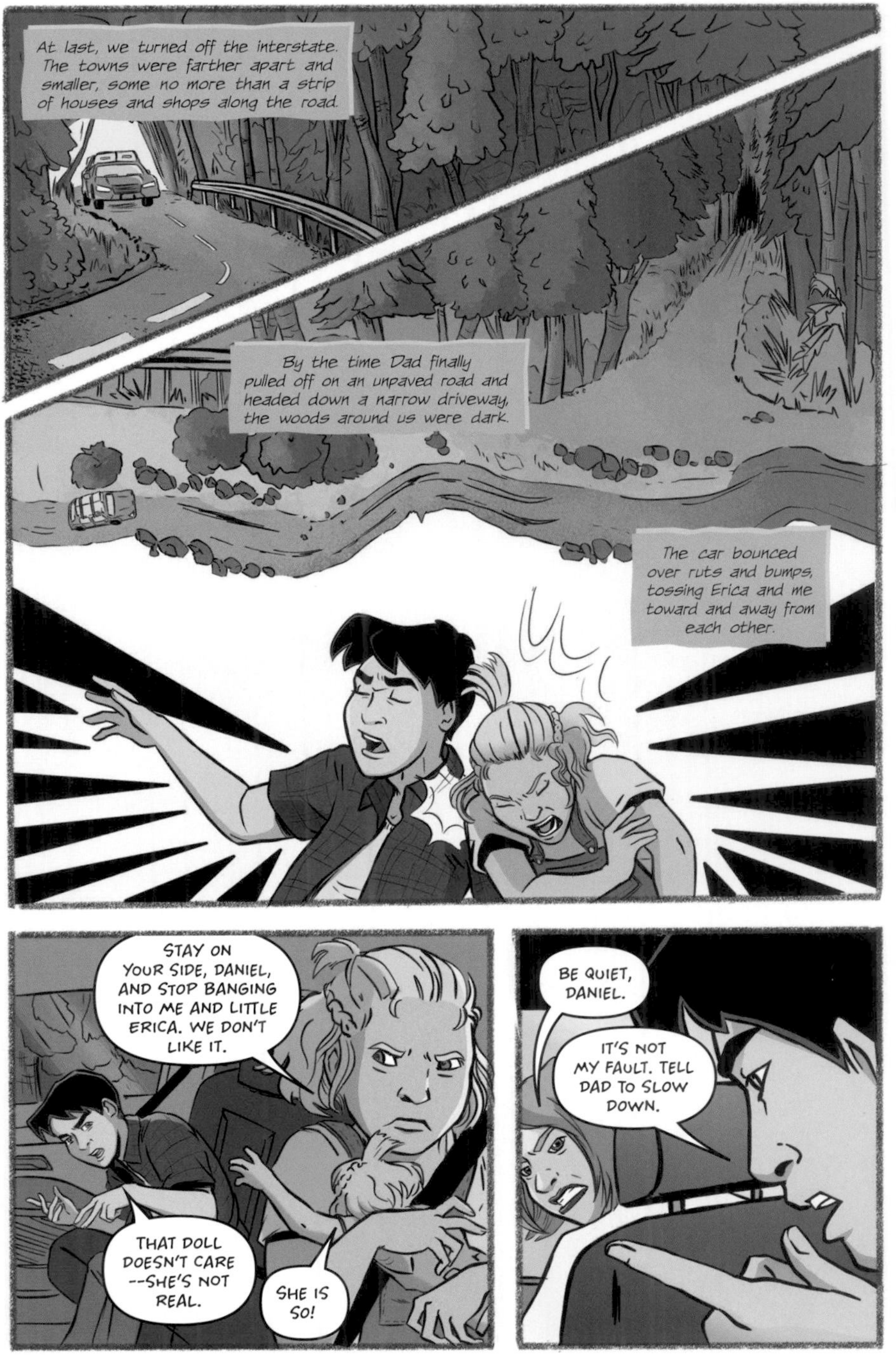
At last, we turned off the interstate. The towns were farther apart and smaller, some no more than a strip of houses and shops along the road.
By the time Dad finally pulled off on an unpaved road and headed down a narrow driveway, the woods around us were dark.
The car bounced over ruts and bumps, tossing Erica and me toward and away from each other.
STAY ON YOUR SIDE, DANIEL, AND STOP BANGING INTO ME AND LITTLE ERICA. WE DON'T LIKE IT.
THAT DOLL DOESN'T CARE --SHE'S NOT REAL.
SHE IS SO!
BE QUIET, DANIEL.
IT'S NOT MY FAULT. TELL DAD TO SLOW DOWN.

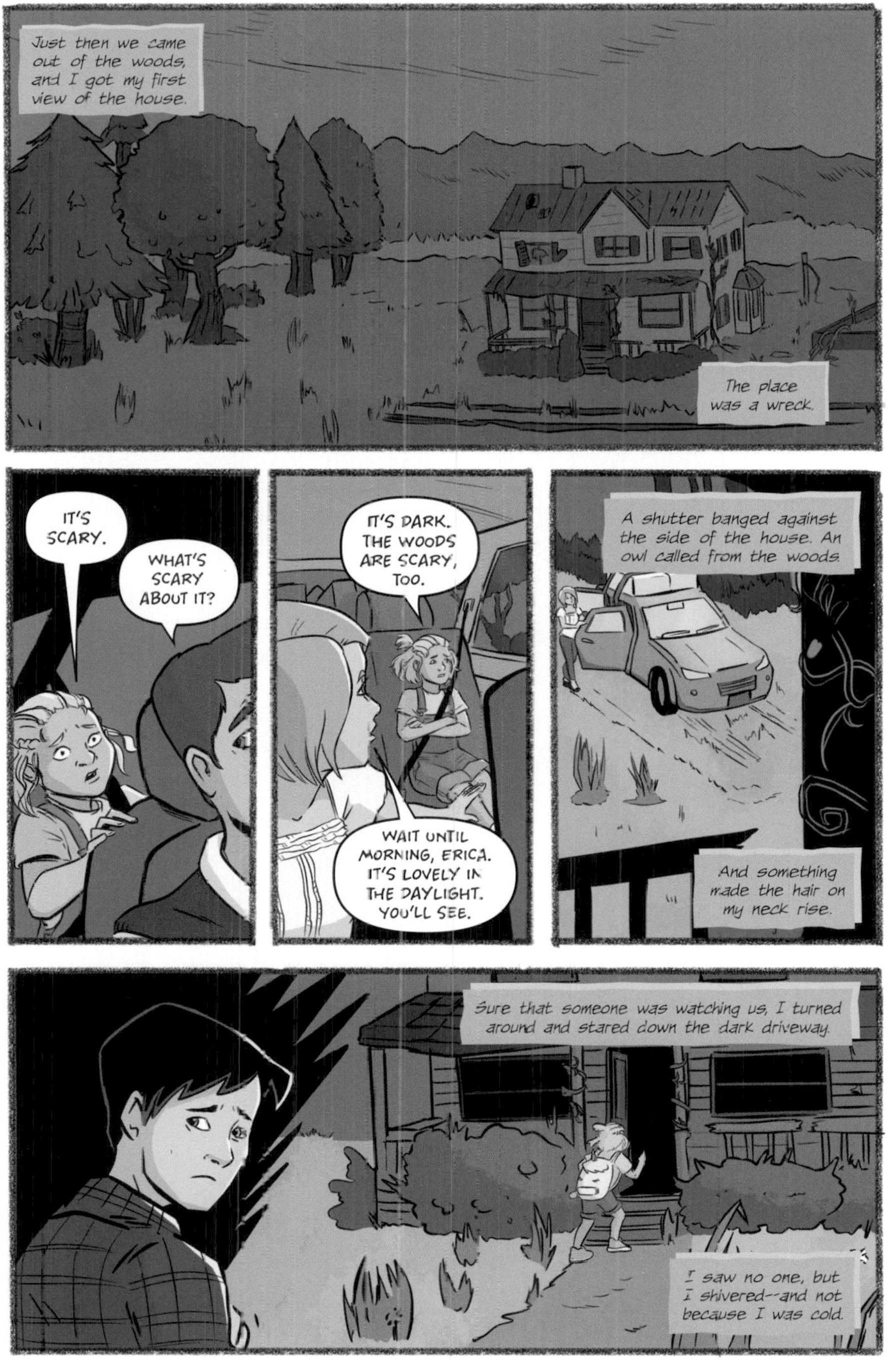

Just then we came out of the woods, and I got my first view of the house.
The place was a wreck.
IT'S SCARY.
WHAT'S SCARY ABOUT IT?
IT'S DARK. THE WOODS ARE SCARY, TOO.
WAIT UNTIL MORNING, ERICA. IT'S LOVELY IN THE DAYLIGHT. YOU'LL SEE.
A shutter banged against the side of the house. An owl called from the woods.
And something made the hair on my neck rise.
Sure that someone was watching us, I turned around and stared down the dark driveway.
I saw no one, but I shivered--and not because I was cold.

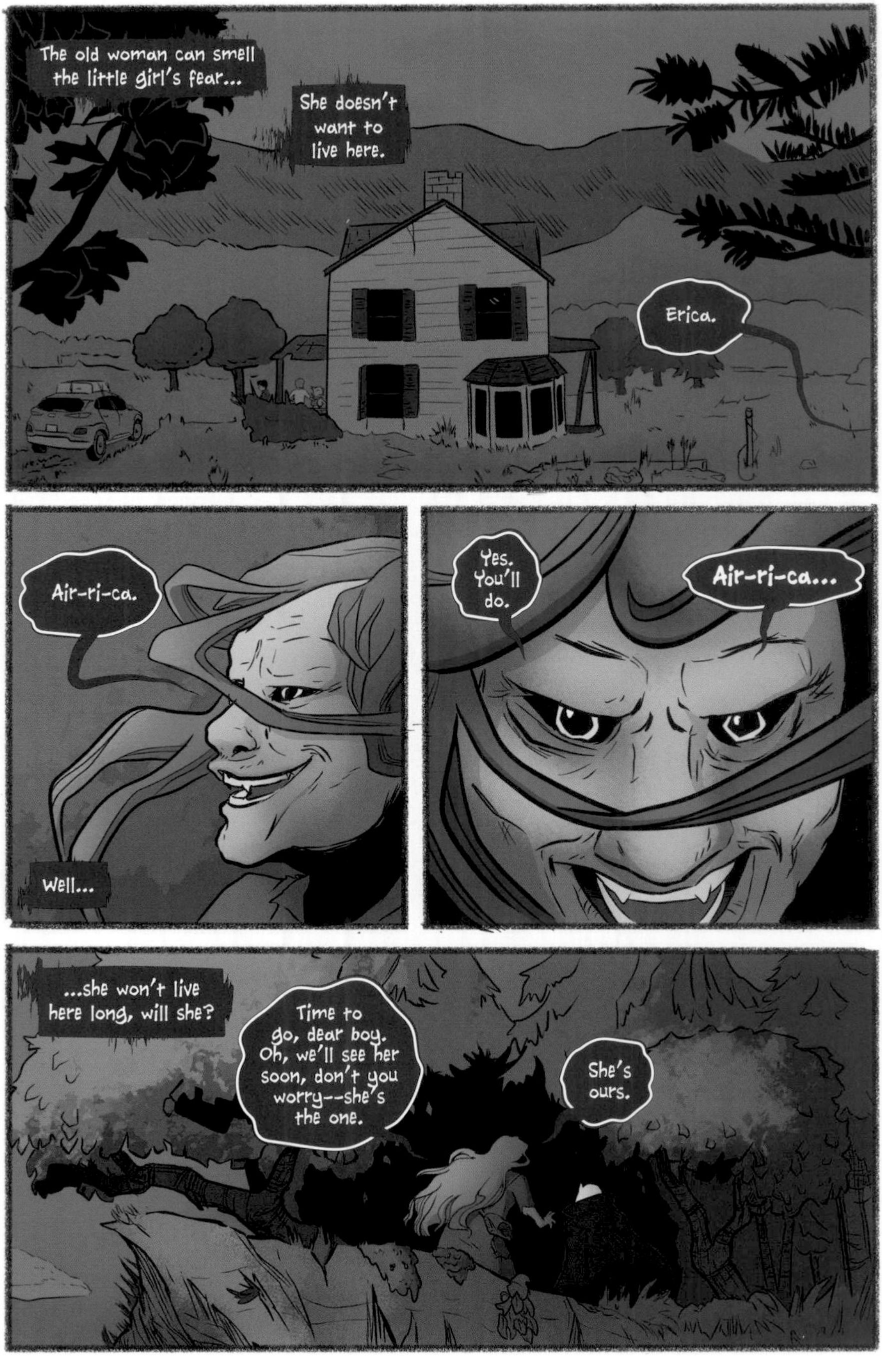
The old woman can smell the little girl's fear...
She doesn't want to live here.
Erica.
Air-ri-ca.
Well...
Yes. You'll do.
Air-ri-ca...
...she won't live here long, will she?
Time to go, dear boy. Oh, we'll see her soon, don't you worry--she's the one.
She's ours.

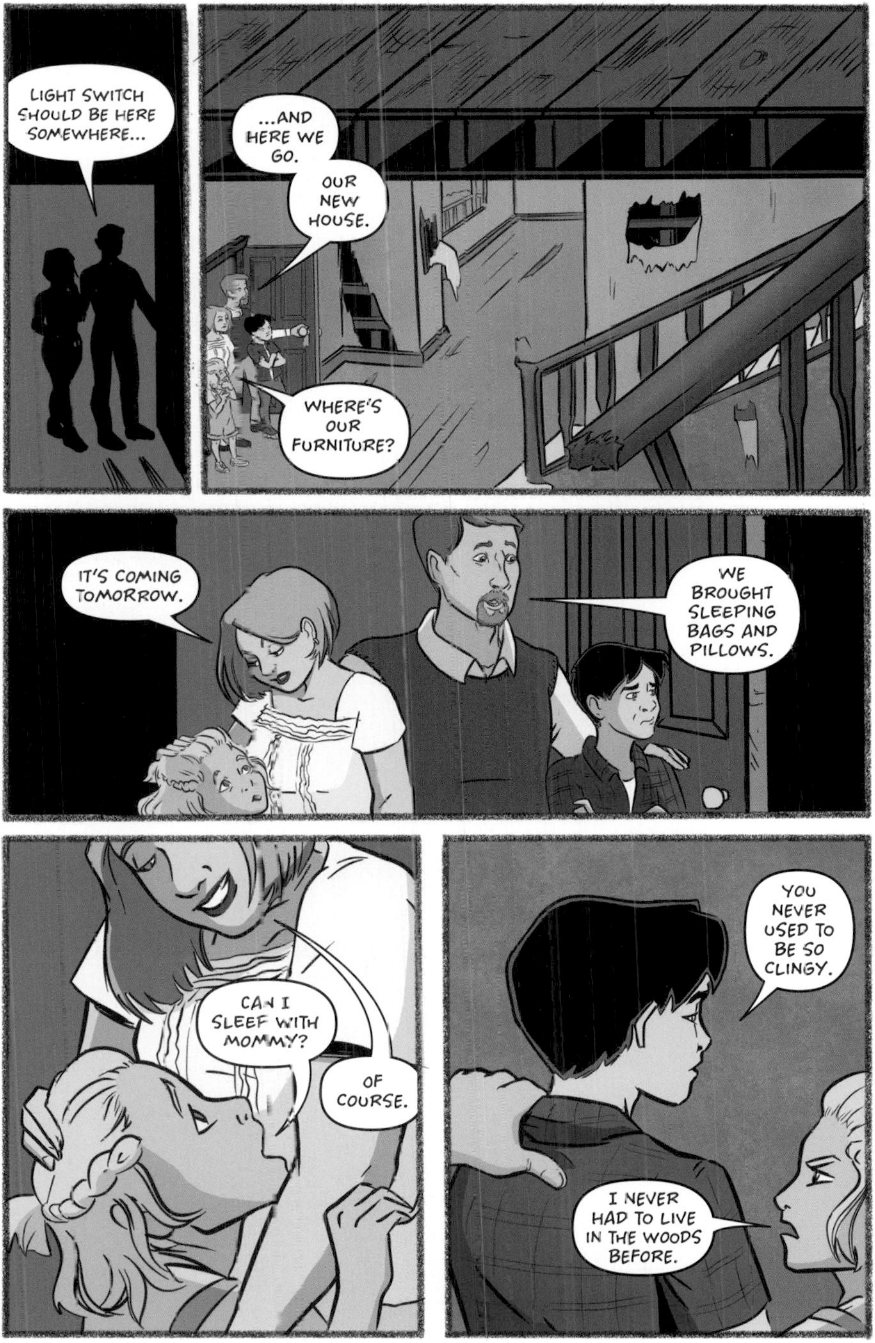
LIGHT SWITCH SHOULD BE HERE SOMEWHERE...
...AND HERE WE GO.
OUR NEW HOUSE.
WHERE'S OUR FURNITURE?
IT'S COMING TOMORROW.
WE BROUGHT SLEEPING BAGS AND PILLOWS.
CAN I SLEEP WITH MOMMY?
OF COURSE.
YOU NEVER USED TO BE SO CLINGY.
I NEVER HAD TO LIVE IN THE WOODS BEFORE.

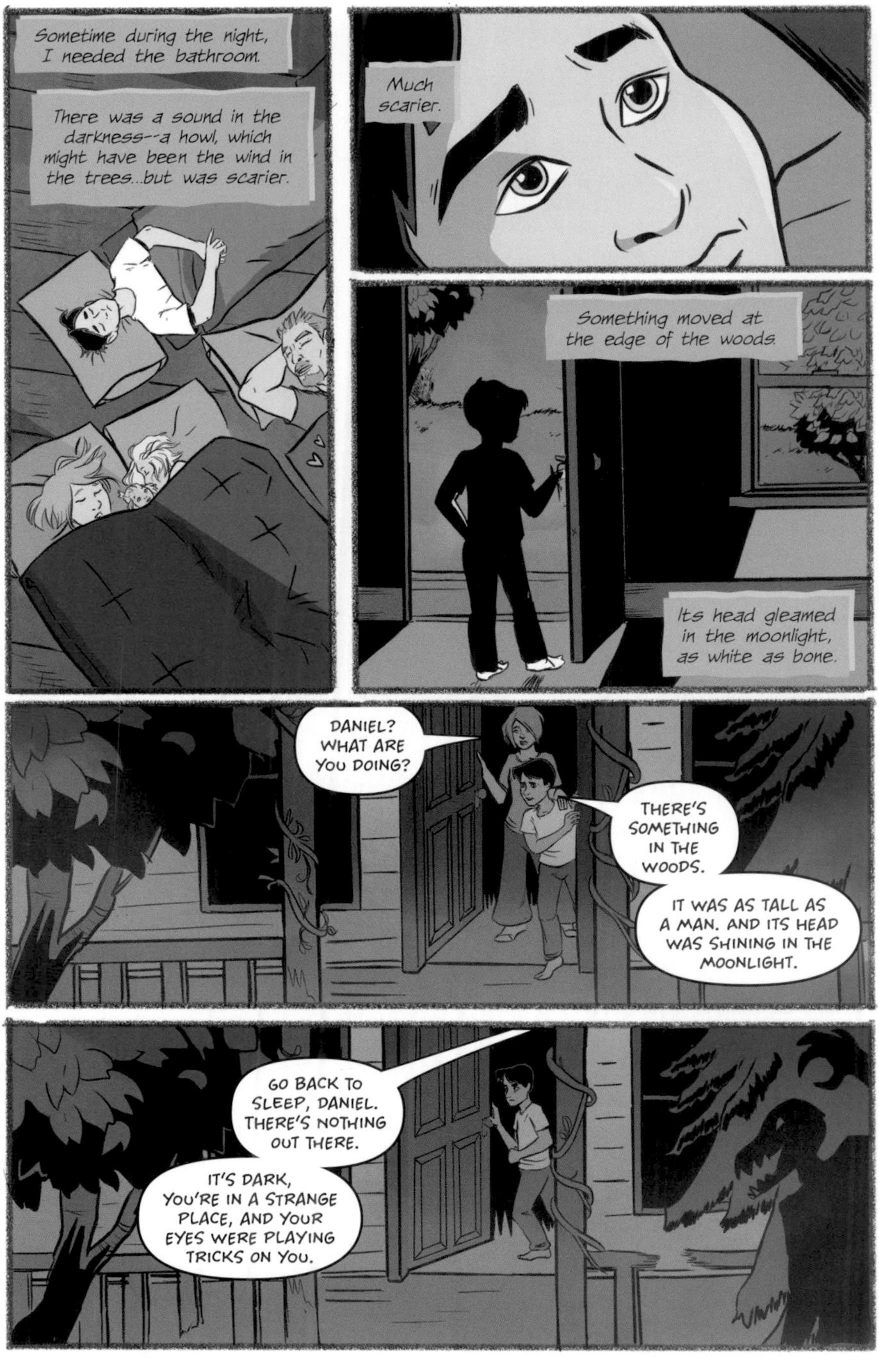
Sometime during the night, I needed the bathroom.
There was a sound in the darkness--a howl, which might have been the wind in the trees...but was scarier.
Much scarier.
Something moved at the edge of the woods.
Its head gleamed in the moonlight, as white as bone.
DANIEL? WHAT ARE YOU DOING?
THERE'S SOMETHING IN THE WOODS.
IT WAS AS TALL AS A MAN. AND ITS HEAD WAS SHINING IN THE MOONLIGHT.
GO BACK TO SLEEP, DANIEL. THERE'S NOTHING OUT THERE.
IT'S DARK, YOU'RE IN A STRANGE PLACE, AND YOUR EYES WERE PLAYING TRICKS ON YOU.

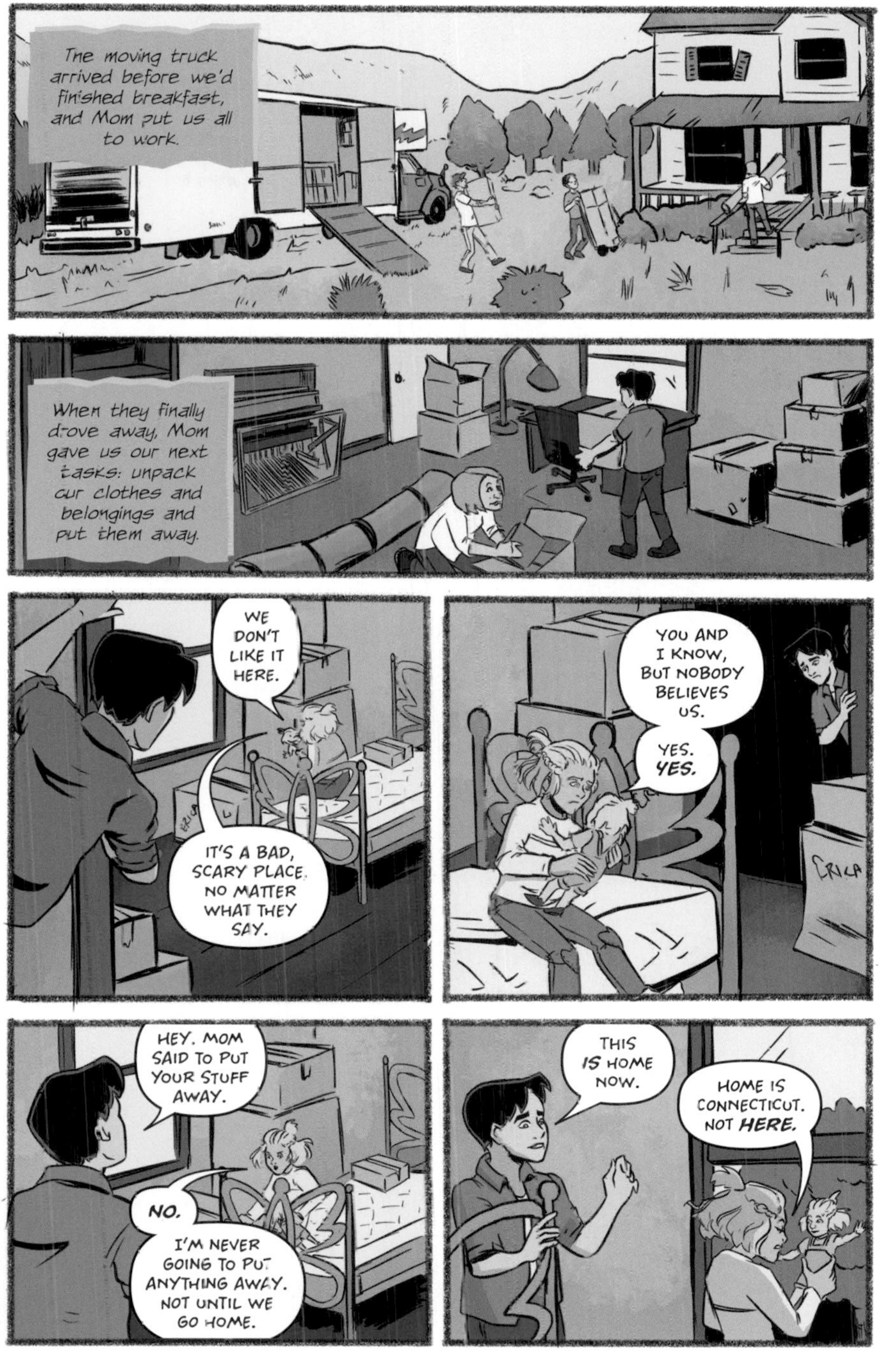

The moving truck arrived before we'd finished breakfast, and Mom put us all to work.
When they finally drove away, Mom gave us our next tasks: unpack our clothes and belongings and put them away.
WE DON'T LIKE IT HERE.
IT'S A BAD, SCARY PLACE. NO MATTER WHAT THEY SAY.
YOU AND I KNOW, BUT NOBODY BELIEVES US.
YES. ***YES.***
ERICA
HEY. MOM SAID TO PUT YOUR STUFF AWAY.
NO.
I'M NEVER GOING TO PUT ANYTHING AWAY. NOT UNTIL WE GO HOME.
THIS ***IS*** HOME NOW.
HOME IS CONNECTICUT. NOT ***HERE.***

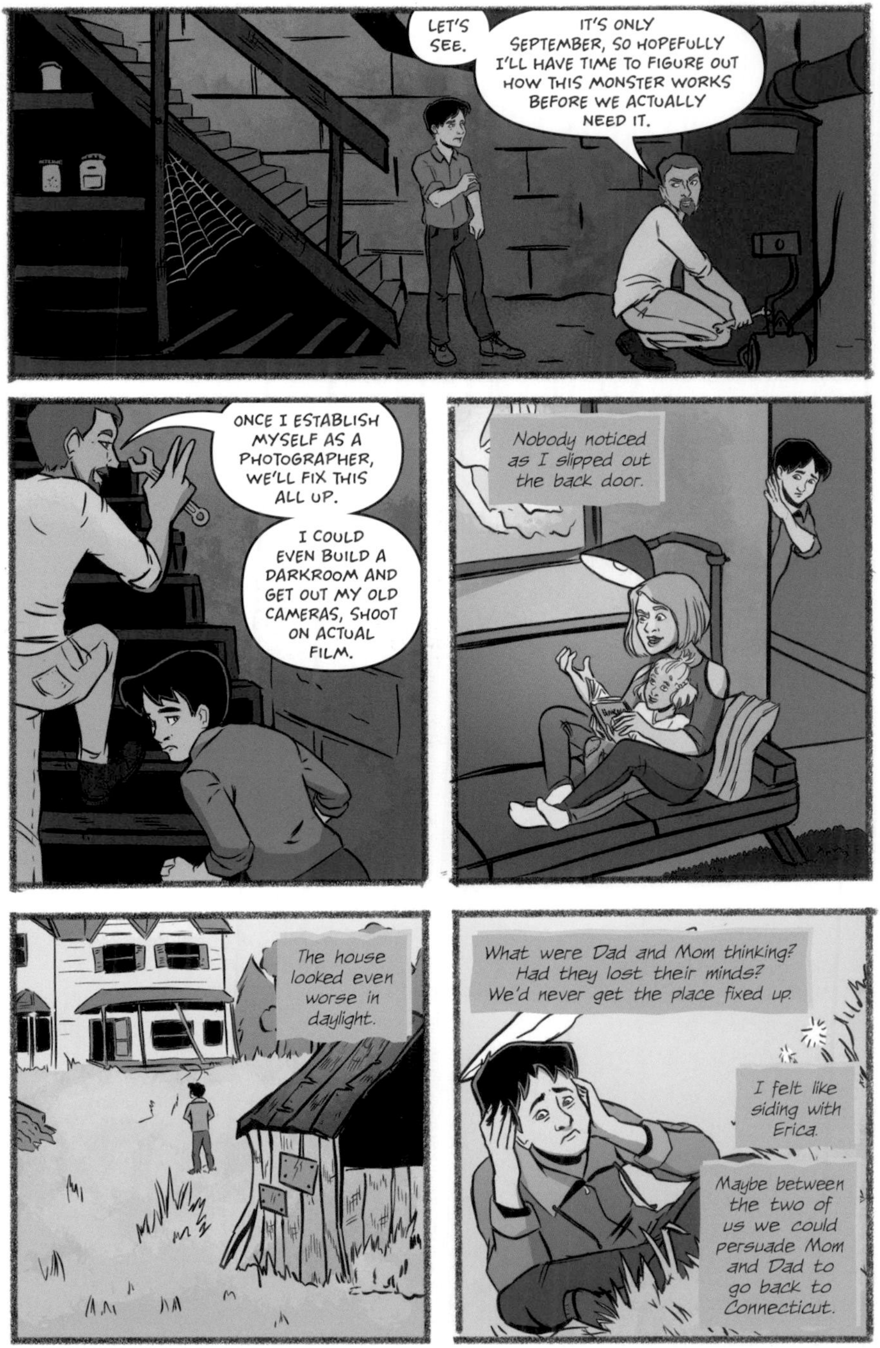
LET'S SEE.
IT'S ONLY SEPTEMBER, SO HOPEFULLY I'LL HAVE TIME TO FIGURE OUT HOW THIS MONSTER WORKS BEFORE WE ACTUALLY NEED IT.
ONCE I ESTABLISH MYSELF AS A PHOTOGRAPHER, WE'LL FIX THIS ALL UP.
I COULD EVEN BUILD A DARKROOM AND GET OUT MY OLD CAMERAS, SHOOT ON ACTUAL FILM.
Nobody noticed as I slipped out the back door.
The house looked even worse in daylight.
What were Dad and Mom thinking? Had they lost their minds? We'd never get the place fixed up.
I felt like siding with Erica.
Maybe between the two of us we could persuade Mom and Dad to go back to Connecticut.

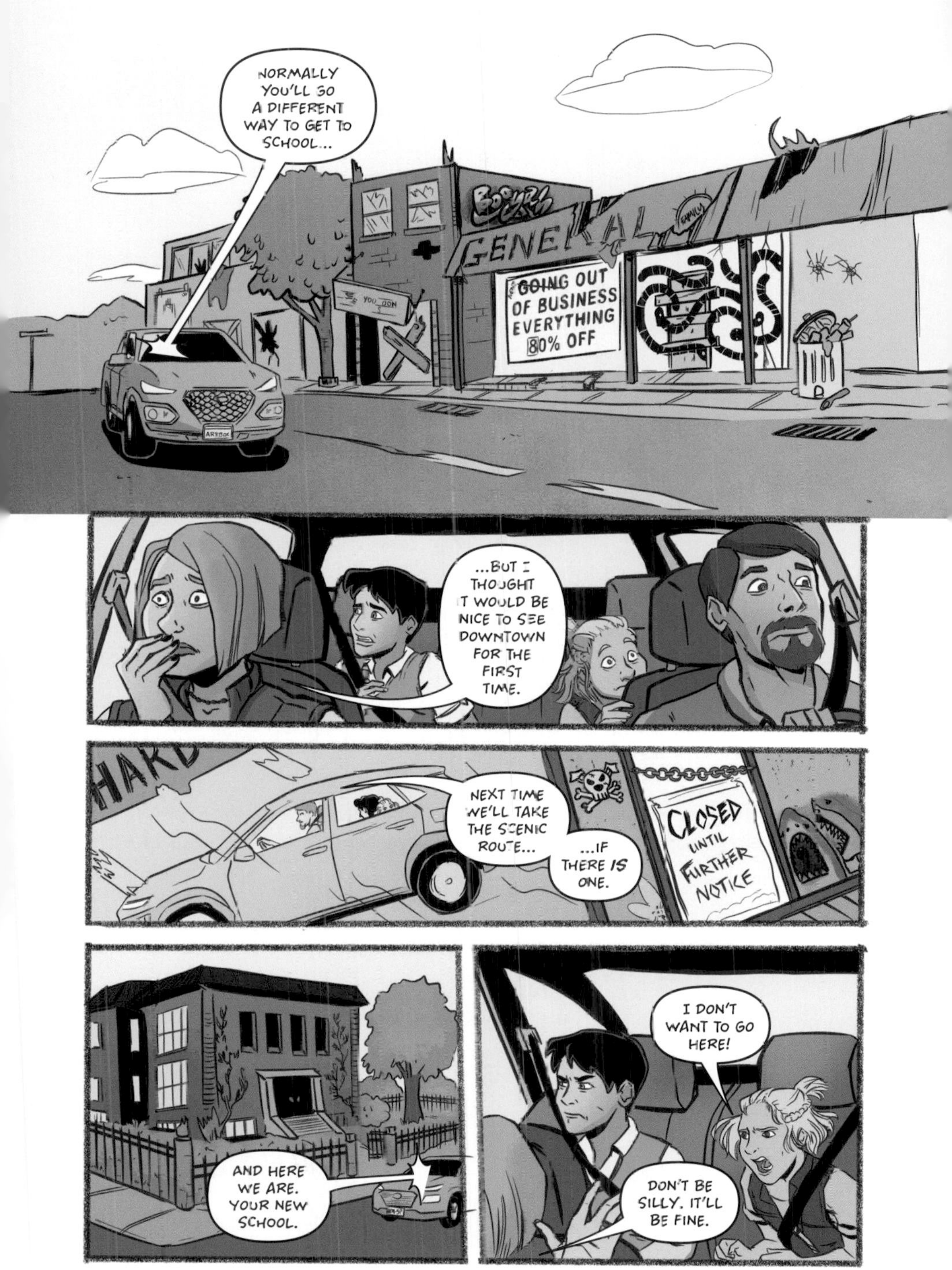
NORMALLY YOU'LL GO A DIFFERENT WAY TO GET TO SCHOOL...
GOING OUT OF BUSINESS EVERYTHING 80% OFF
...BUT I THOUGHT IT WOULD BE NICE TO SEE DOWNTOWN FOR THE FIRST TIME.
NEXT TIME WE'LL TAKE THE SCENIC ROUTE...
...IF THERE *IS* ONE.
CLOSED UNTIL FURTHER NOTICE
AND HERE WE ARE. YOUR NEW SCHOOL.
I DON'T WANT TO GO HERE!
DON'T BE SILLY. IT'LL BE FINE.

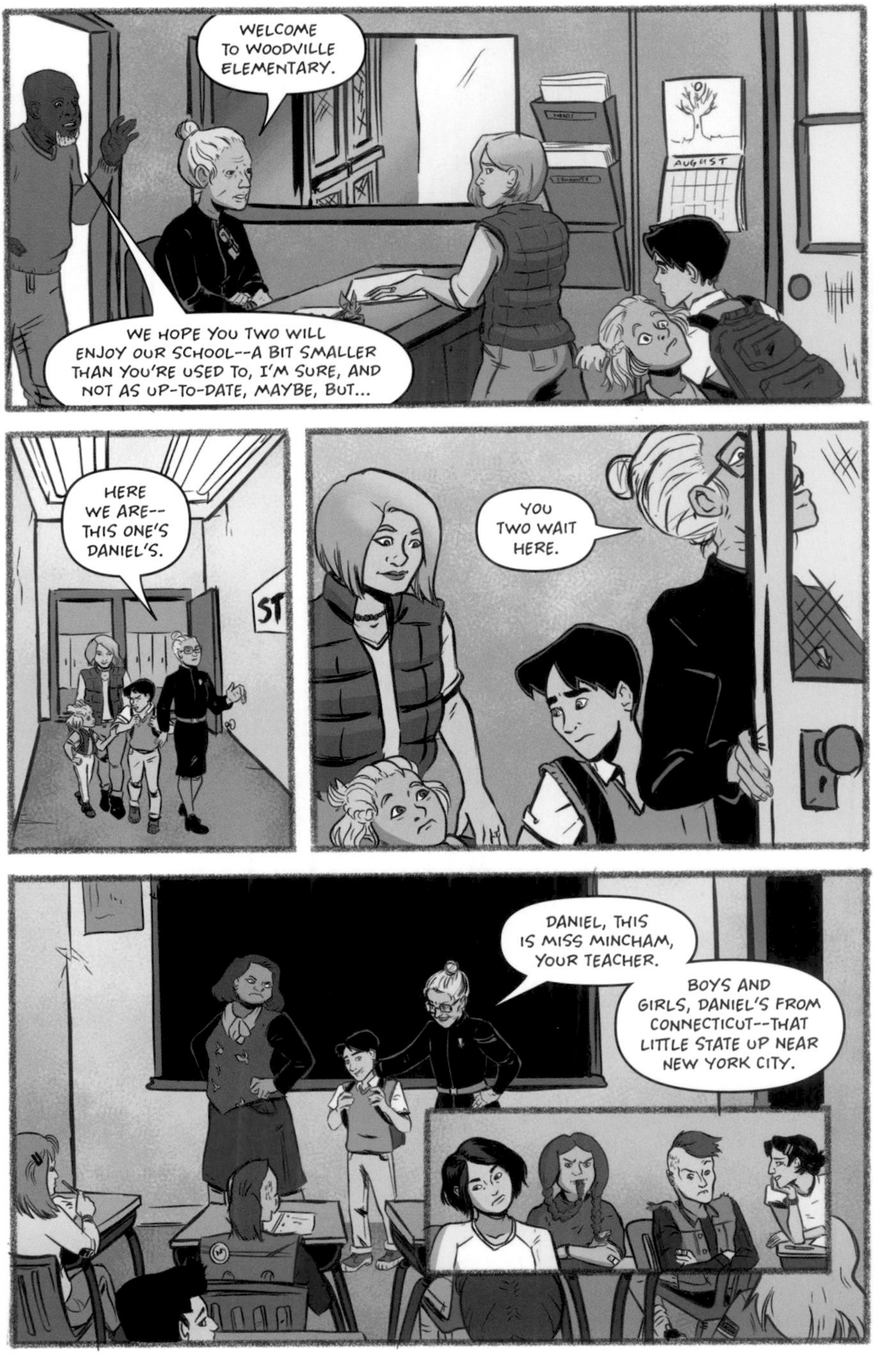
WELCOME TO WOODVILLE ELEMENTARY.
WE HOPE YOU TWO WILL ENJOY OUR SCHOOL--A BIT SMALLER THAN YOU'RE USED TO, I'M SURE, AND NOT AS UP-TO-DATE, MAYBE, BUT...
AUGUST
HERE WE ARE--THIS ONE'S DANIEL'S.
YOU TWO WAIT HERE.
DANIEL, THIS IS MISS MINCHAM, YOUR TEACHER.
BOYS AND GIRLS, DANIEL'S FROM CONNECTICUT--THAT LITTLE STATE UP NEAR NEW YORK CITY.

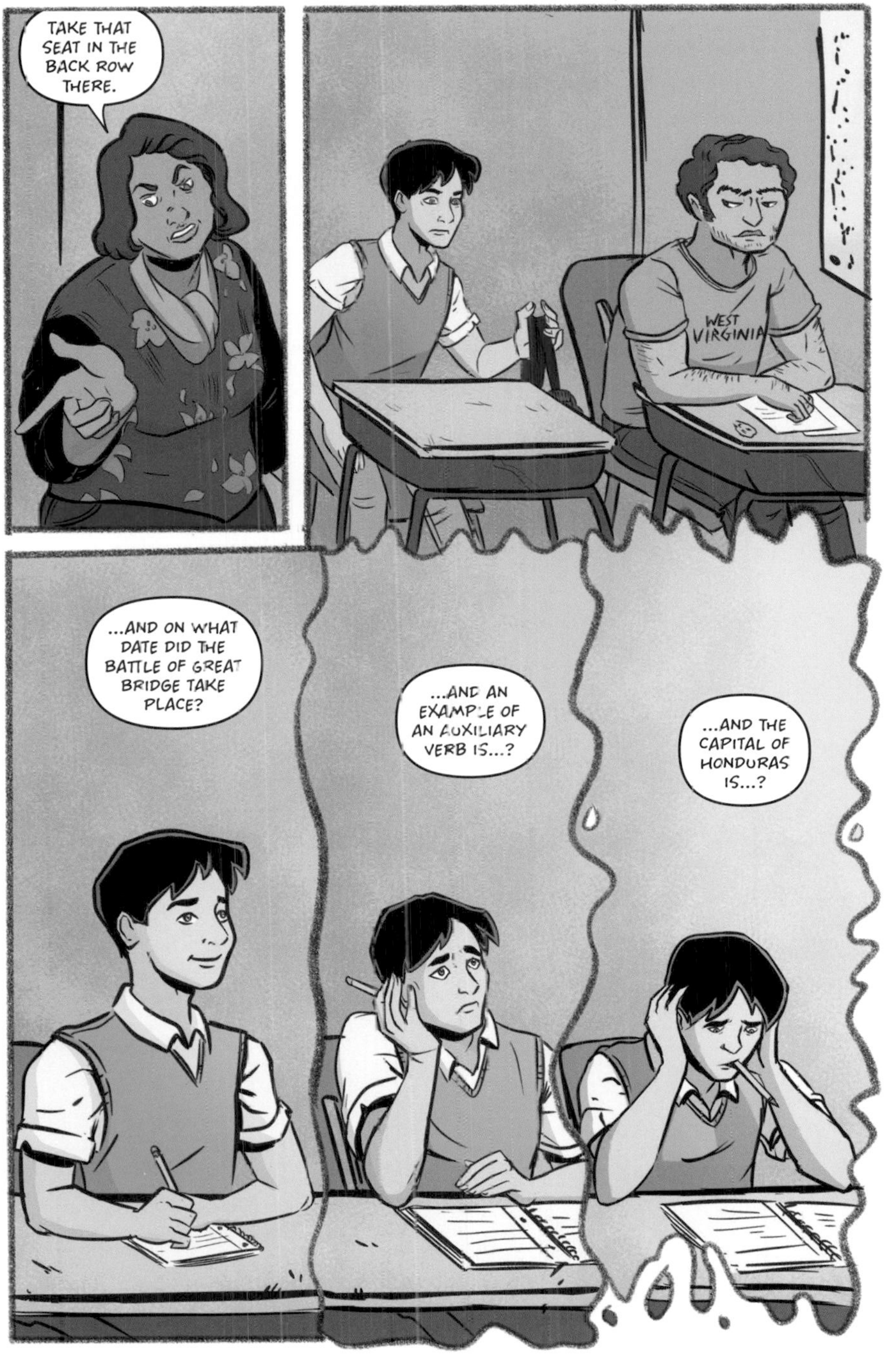
TAKE THAT SEAT IN THE BACK ROW THERE.
WEST VIRGINIA
...AND ON WHAT DATE DID THE BATTLE OF GREAT BRIDGE TAKE PLACE?
...AND AN EXAMPLE OF AN AUXILIARY VERB IS...?
...AND THE CAPITAL OF HONDURAS IS...?

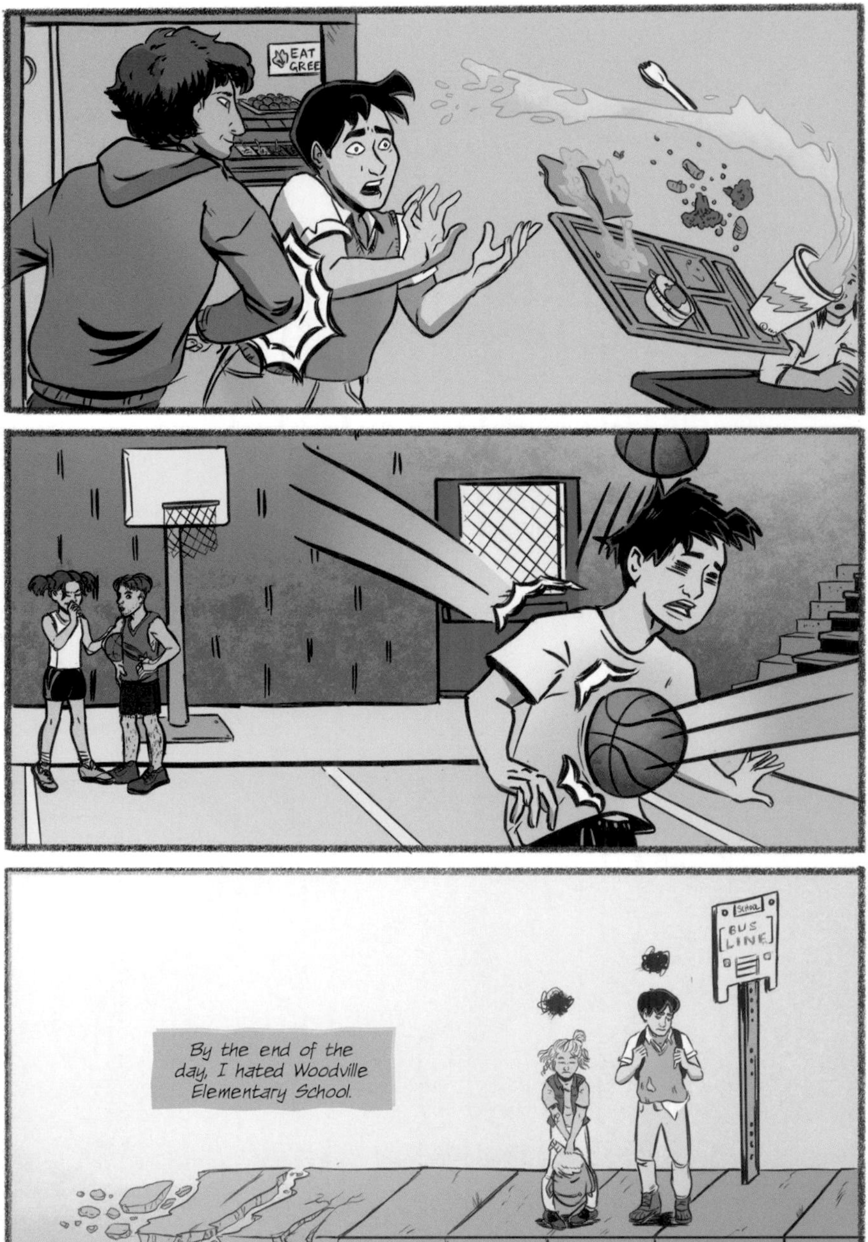
EAT
GREE
BUS
LINE
By the end of the day, I hated Woodville Elementary School.

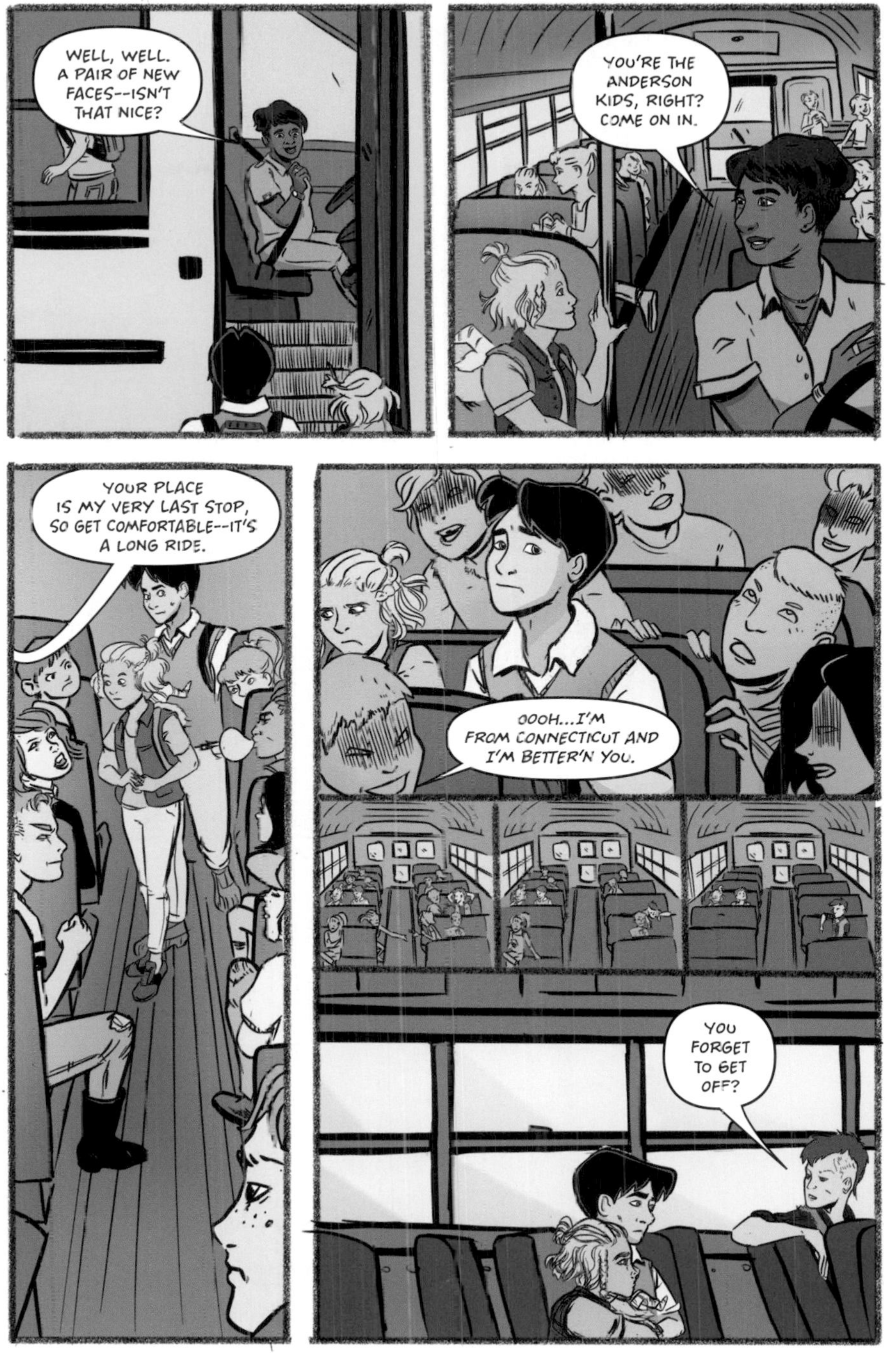
WELL, WELL. A PAIR OF NEW FACES--ISN'T THAT NICE?
YOU'RE THE ANDERSON KIDS, RIGHT? COME ON IN.
YOUR PLACE IS MY VERY LAST STOP, SO GET COMFORTABLE--IT'S A LONG RIDE.
OOOH...I'M FROM CONNECTICUT AND I'M BETTER'N YOU.
YOU FORGET TO GET OFF?

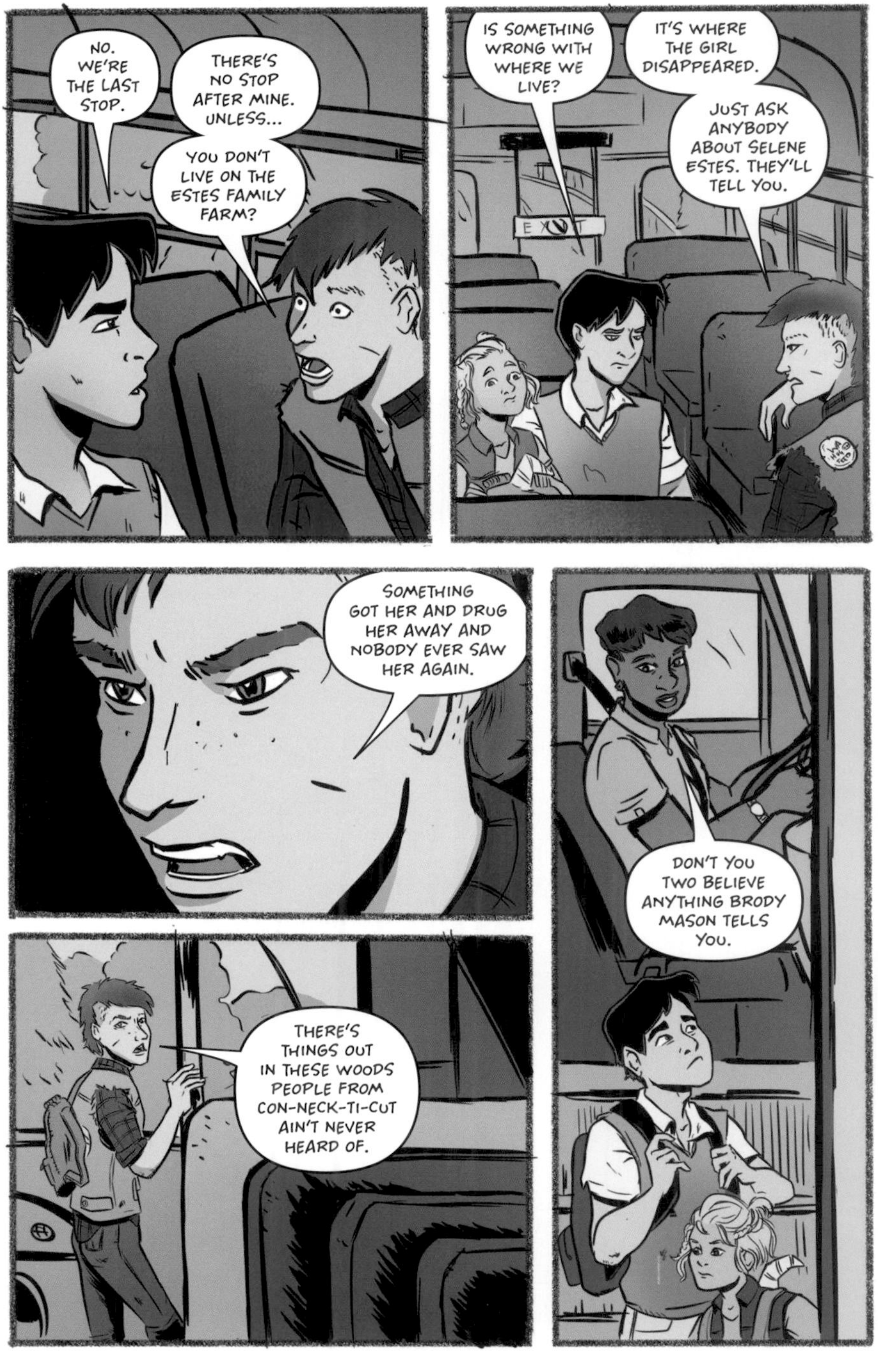
NO. WE'RE THE LAST STOP.
THERE'S NO STOP AFTER MINE. UNLESS...
YOU DON'T LIVE ON THE ESTES FAMILY FARM?
IS SOMETHING WRONG WITH WHERE WE LIVE?
IT'S WHERE THE GIRL DISAPPEARED.
JUST ASK ANYBODY ABOUT SELENE ESTES. THEY'LL TELL YOU.
SOMETHING GOT HER AND DRUG HER AWAY AND NOBODY EVER SAW HER AGAIN.
DON'T YOU TWO BELIEVE ANYTHING BRODY MASON TELLS YOU.
THERE'S THINGS OUT IN THESE WOODS PEOPLE FROM CON-NECK-TI-CUT AIN'T NEVER HEARD OF.

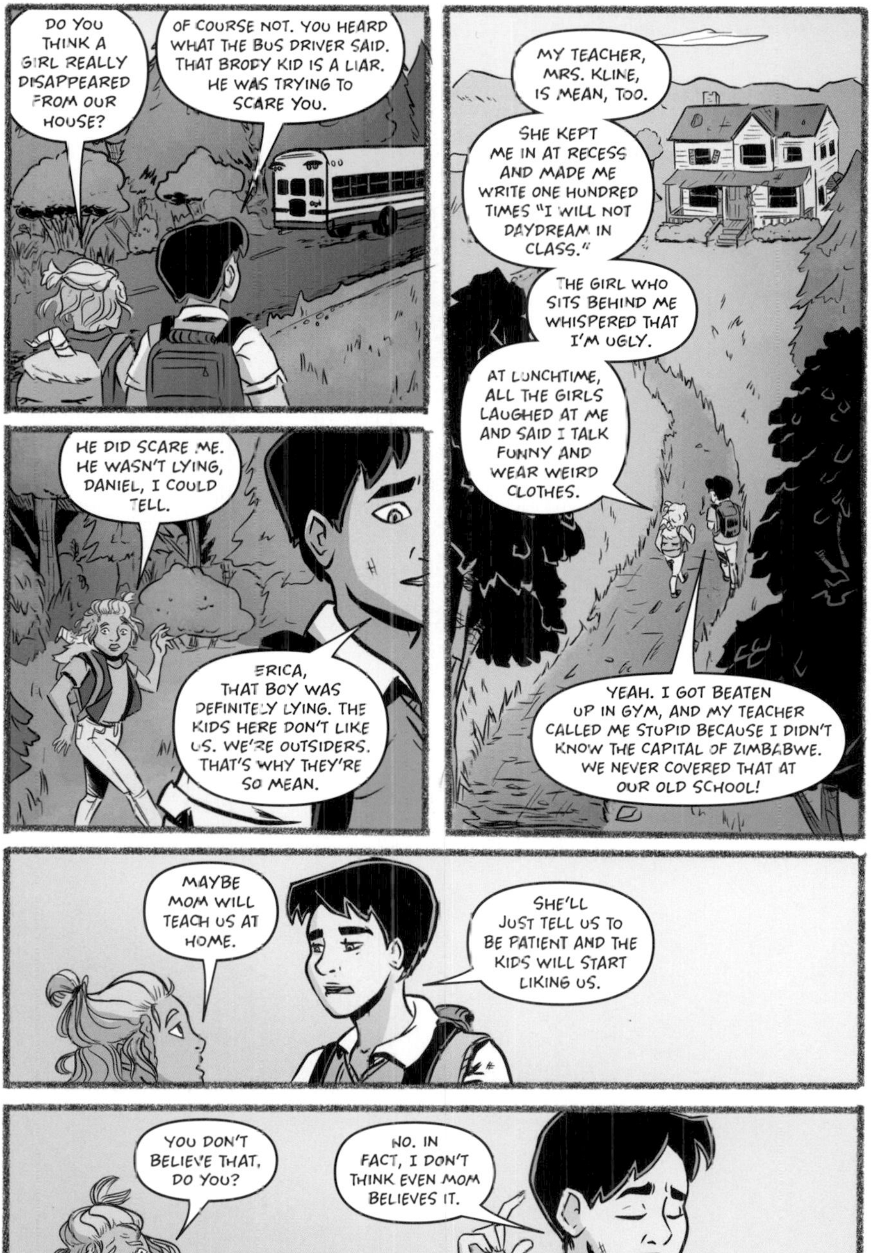
DO YOU THINK A GIRL REALLY DISAPPEARED FROM OUR HOUSE?
OF COURSE NOT. YOU HEARD WHAT THE BUS DRIVER SAID. THAT BRODY KID IS A LIAR. HE WAS TRYING TO SCARE YOU.
HE DID SCARE ME. HE WASN'T LYING, DANIEL, I COULD TELL.
ERICA, THAT BOY WAS DEFINITELY LYING. THE KIDS HERE DON'T LIKE US. WE'RE OUTSIDERS. THAT'S WHY THEY'RE SO MEAN.
MY TEACHER, MRS. KLINE, IS MEAN, TOO.
SHE KEPT ME IN AT RECESS AND MADE ME WRITE ONE HUNDRED TIMES "I WILL NOT DAYDREAM IN CLASS."
THE GIRL WHO SITS BEHIND ME WHISPERED THAT I'M UGLY.
AT LUNCHTIME, ALL THE GIRLS LAUGHED AT ME AND SAID I TALK FUNNY AND WEAR WEIRD CLOTHES.
YEAH. I GOT BEATEN UP IN GYM, AND MY TEACHER CALLED ME STUPID BECAUSE I DIDN'T KNOW THE CAPITAL OF ZIMBABWE. WE NEVER COVERED THAT AT OUR OLD SCHOOL!
MAYBE MOM WILL TEACH US AT HOME.
SHE'LL JUST TELL US TO BE PATIENT AND THE KIDS WILL START LIKING US.
YOU DON'T BELIEVE THAT, DO YOU?
NO. IN FACT, I DON'T THINK EVEN MOM BELIEVES IT.

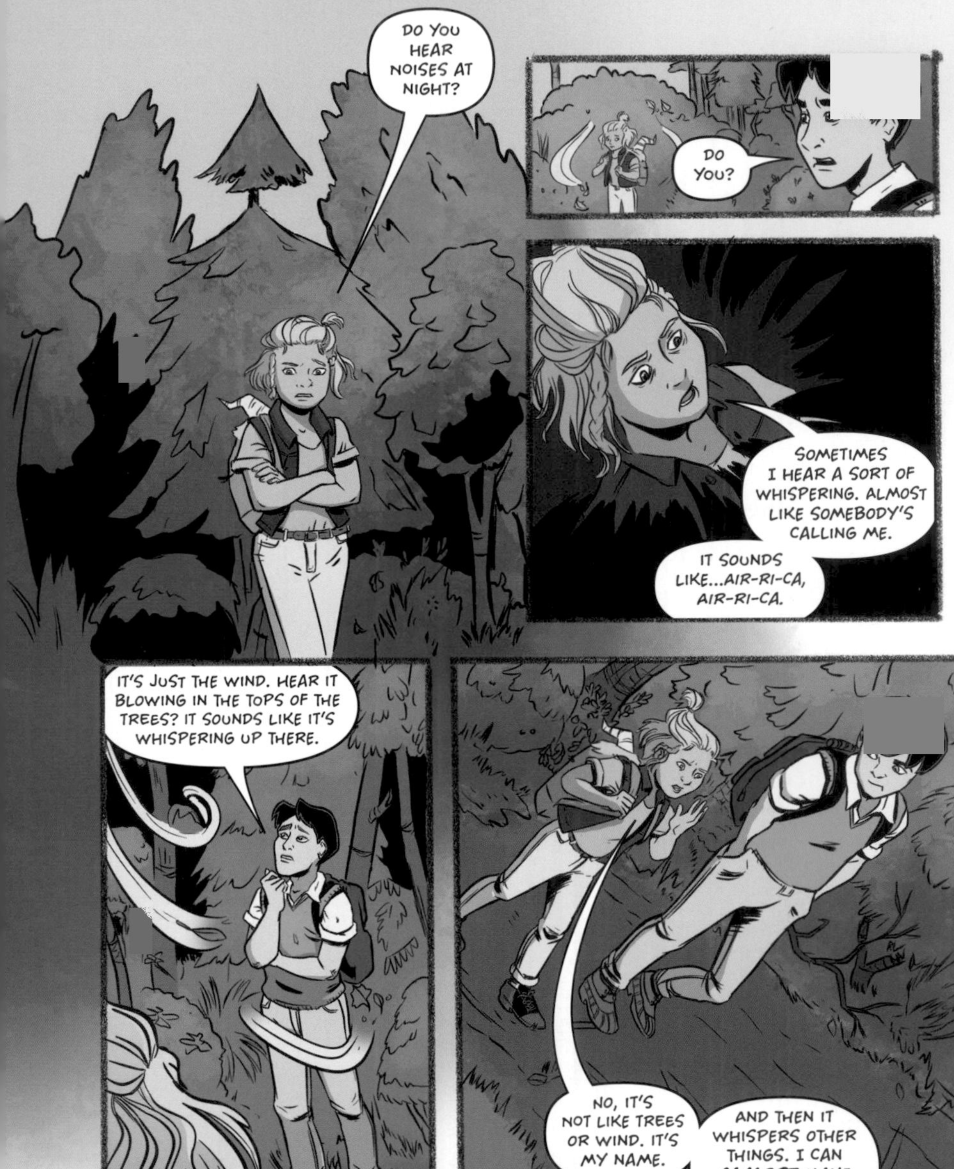
DO YOU HEAR NOISES AT NIGHT?
DO YOU?
SOMETIMES I HEAR A SORT OF WHISPERING. ALMOST LIKE SOMEBODY'S CALLING ME.
IT SOUNDS LIKE...AIR-RI-CA, AIR-RI-CA.
IT'S JUST THE WIND. HEAR IT BLOWING IN THE TOPS OF THE TREES? IT SOUNDS LIKE IT'S WHISPERING UP THERE.
NO, IT'S NOT LIKE TREES OR WIND. IT'S MY NAME.
AND THEN IT WHISPERS OTHER THINGS. I CAN ***ALMOST*** MAKE OUT THE WORDS, BUT NOT QUITE.
NOT QUITE.

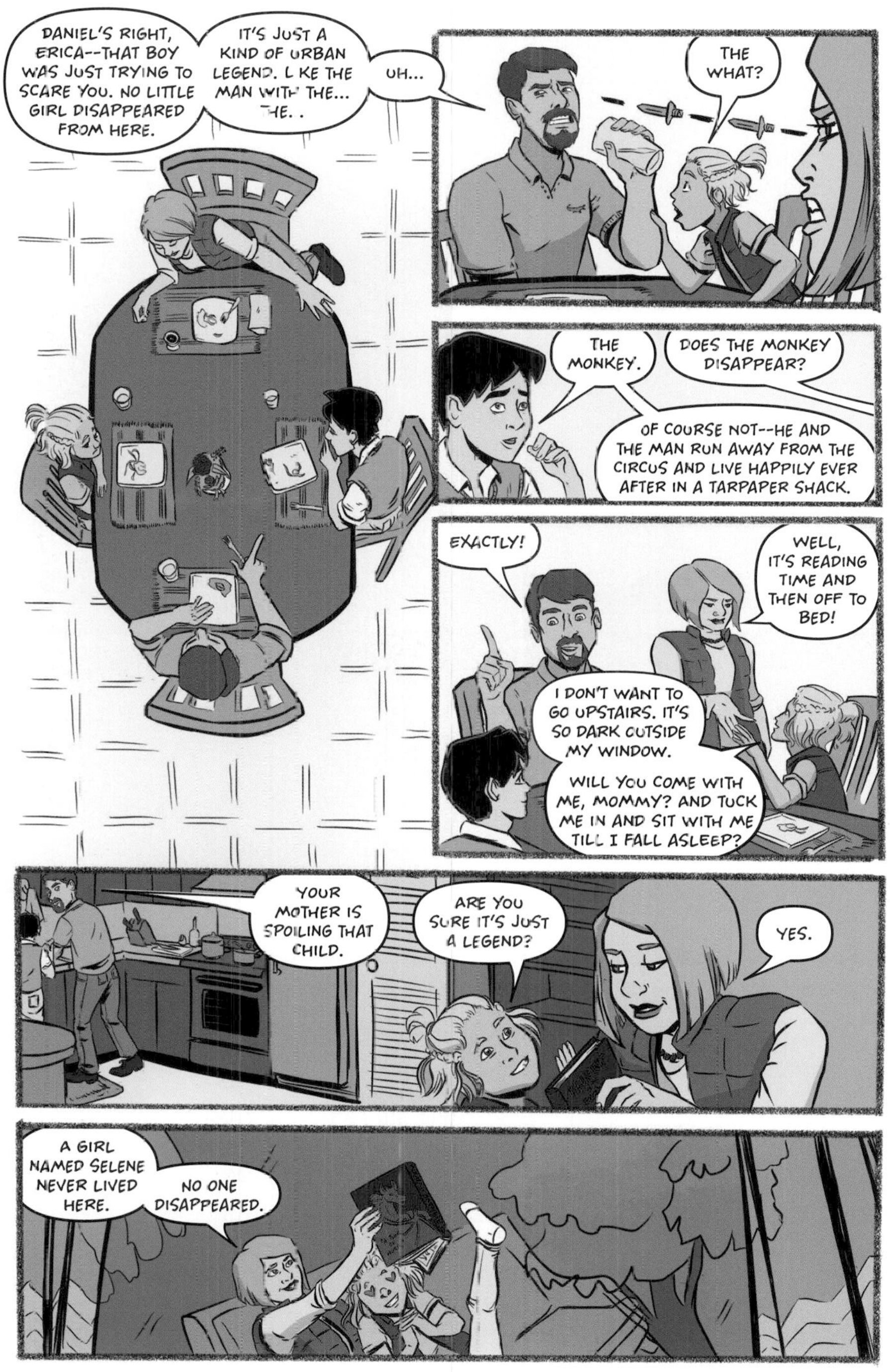
DANIEL'S RIGHT, ERICA--THAT BOY WAS JUST TRYING TO SCARE YOU. NO LITTLE GIRL DISAPPEARED FROM HERE.
IT'S JUST A KIND OF URBAN LEGEND. L KE THE MAN WITH THE... THE. .
UH...
THE WHAT?
THE MONKEY.
DOES THE MONKEY DISAPPEAR?
OF COURSE NOT--HE AND THE MAN RUN AWAY FROM THE CIRCUS AND LIVE HAPPILY EVER AFTER IN A TARPAPER SHACK.
EXACTLY!
WELL, IT'S READING TIME AND THEN OFF TO BED!
I DON'T WANT TO GO UPSTAIRS. IT'S SO DARK OUTSIDE MY WINDOW.
WILL YOU COME WITH ME, MOMMY? AND TUCK ME IN AND SIT WITH ME TILL I FALL ASLEEP?
YOUR MOTHER IS SPOILING THAT CHILD.
ARE YOU SURE IT'S JUST A LEGEND?
YES.
A GIRL NAMED SELENE NEVER LIVED HERE.
NO ONE DISAPPEARED.

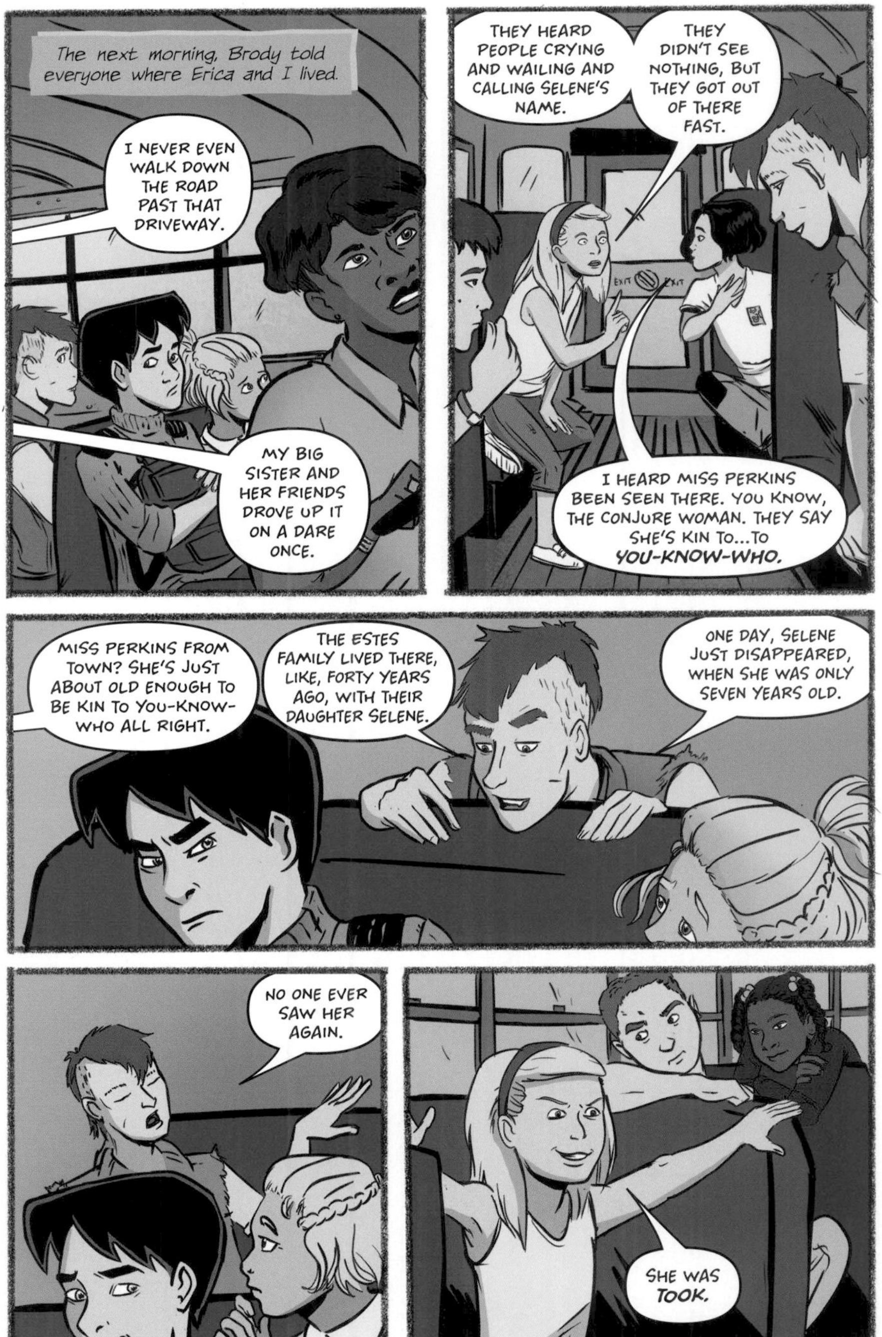
The next morning, Brody told everyone where Erica and I lived.
I NEVER EVEN WALK DOWN THE ROAD PAST THAT DRIVEWAY.
MY BIG SISTER AND HER FRIENDS DROVE UP IT ON A DARE ONCE.
THEY HEARD PEOPLE CRYING AND WAILING AND CALLING SELENE'S NAME.
THEY DIDN'T SEE NOTHING, BUT THEY GOT OUT OF THERE FAST.
EXIT
EXIT
I HEARD MISS PERKINS BEEN SEEN THERE. YOU KNOW, THE CONJURE WOMAN. THEY SAY SHE'S KIN TO...TO ***YOU-KNOW-WHO.***
MISS PERKINS FROM TOWN? SHE'S JUST ABOUT OLD ENOUGH TO BE KIN TO YOU-KNOW-WHO ALL RIGHT.
THE ESTES FAMILY LIVED THERE, LIKE, FORTY YEARS AGO, WITH THEIR DAUGHTER SELENE.
ONE DAY, SELENE JUST DISAPPEARED, WHEN SHE WAS ONLY SEVEN YEARS OLD.
NO ONE EVER SAW HER AGAIN.
SHE WAS ***TOOK.***

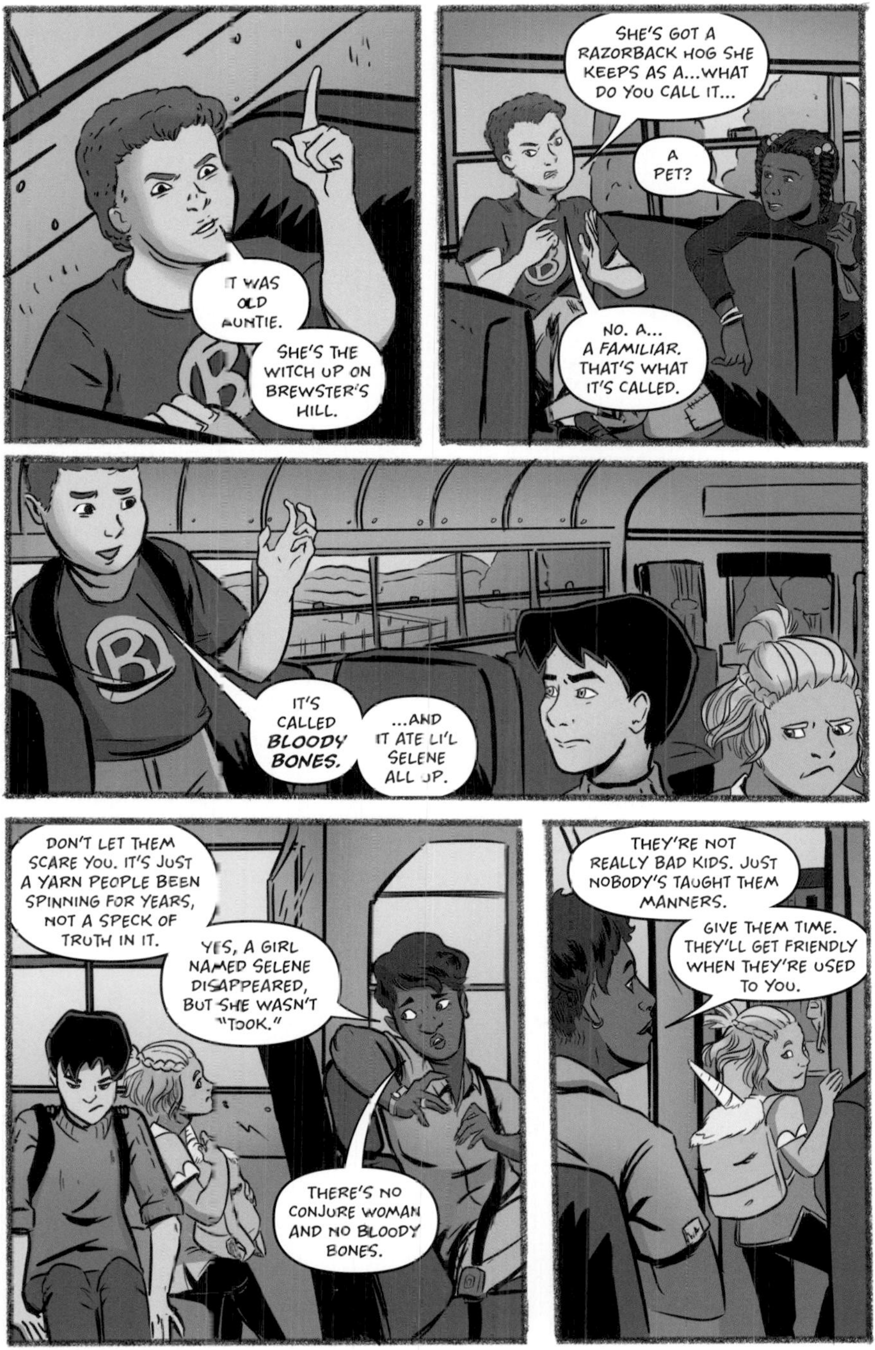
IT WAS OLD AUNTIE.
SHE'S THE WITCH UP ON BREWSTER'S HILL.
SHE'S GOT A RAZORBACK HOG SHE KEEPS AS A...WHAT DO YOU CALL IT...
A PET?
NO. A... A FAMILIAR. THAT'S WHAT IT'S CALLED.
IT'S CALLED *BLOODY BONES.*
...AND IT ATE LI'L SELENE ALL UP.
DON'T LET THEM SCARE YOU. IT'S JUST A YARN PEOPLE BEEN SPINNING FOR YEARS, NOT A SPECK OF TRUTH IN IT.
YES, A GIRL NAMED SELENE DISAPPEARED, BUT SHE WASN'T "TOOK."
THERE'S NO CONJURE WOMAN AND NO BLOODY BONES.
THEY'RE NOT REALLY BAD KIDS. JUST NOBODY'S TAUGHT THEM MANNERS.
GIVE THEM TIME. THEY'LL GET FRIENDLY WHEN THEY'RE USED TO YOU.

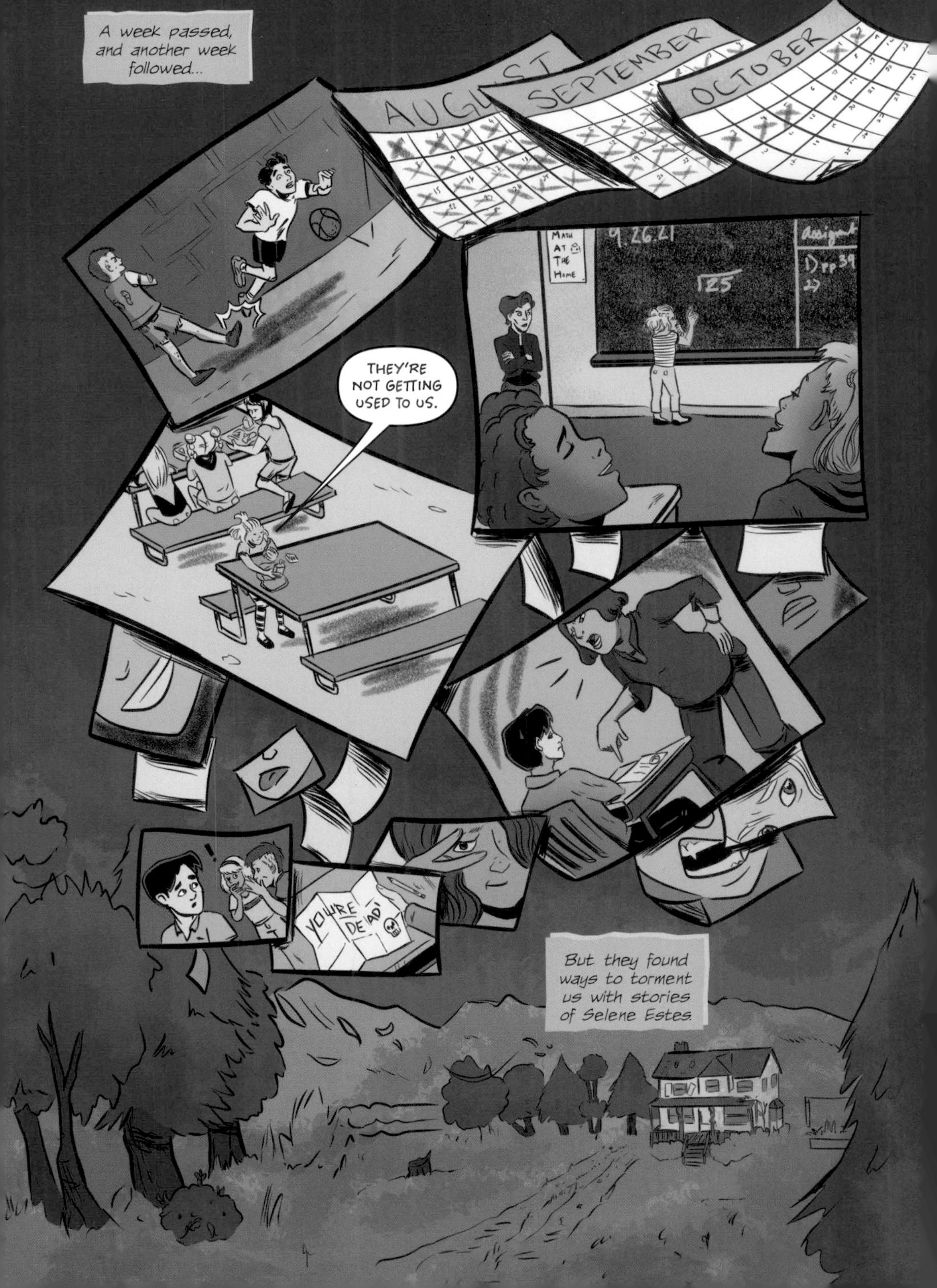
A week passed, and another week followed...
AUGUST
SEPTEMBER
OCTOBER
MATH AT THE HOME
9.26.21
√25
THEY'RE NOT GETTING USED TO US.
YOU'RE DEAD
But they found ways to torment us with stories of Selene Estes.

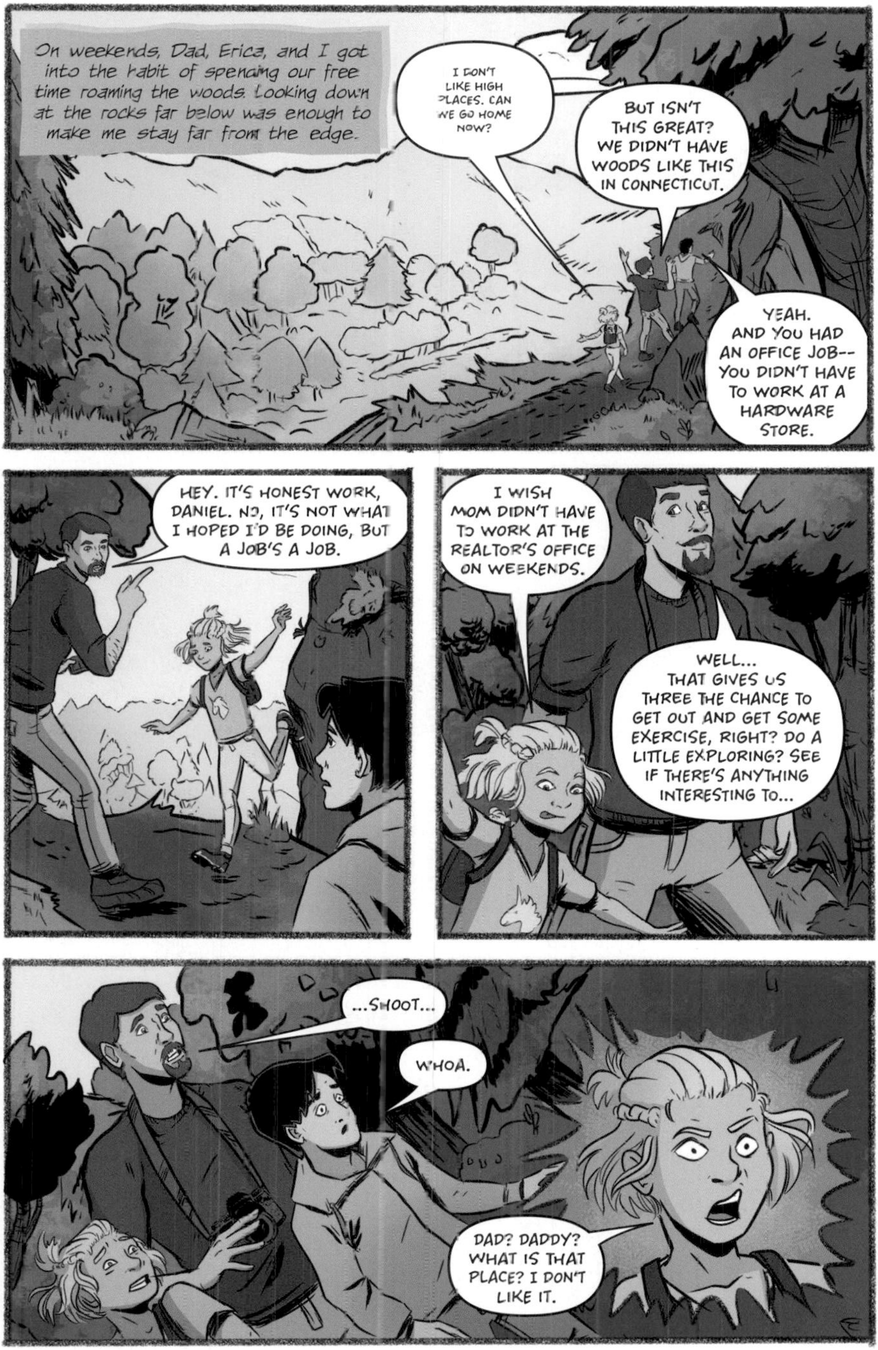
On weekends, Dad, Erica, and I got into the habit of spending our free time roaming the woods. Looking down at the rocks far below was enough to make me stay far from the edge.
I DON'T LIKE HIGH PLACES. CAN WE GO HOME NOW?
BUT ISN'T THIS GREAT? WE DIDN'T HAVE WOODS LIKE THIS IN CONNECTICUT.
YEAH. AND YOU HAD AN OFFICE JOB-- YOU DIDN'T HAVE TO WORK AT A HARDWARE STORE.
HEY. IT'S HONEST WORK, DANIEL. NO, IT'S NOT WHAT I HOPED I'D BE DOING, BUT A JOB'S A JOB.
I WISH MOM DIDN'T HAVE TO WORK AT THE REALTOR'S OFFICE ON WEEKENDS.
WELL... THAT GIVES US THREE THE CHANCE TO GET OUT AND GET SOME EXERCISE, RIGHT? DO A LITTLE EXPLORING? SEE IF THERE'S ANYTHING INTERESTING TO...
...SHOOT...
WHOA.
DAD? DADDY? WHAT IS THAT PLACE? I DON'T LIKE IT.

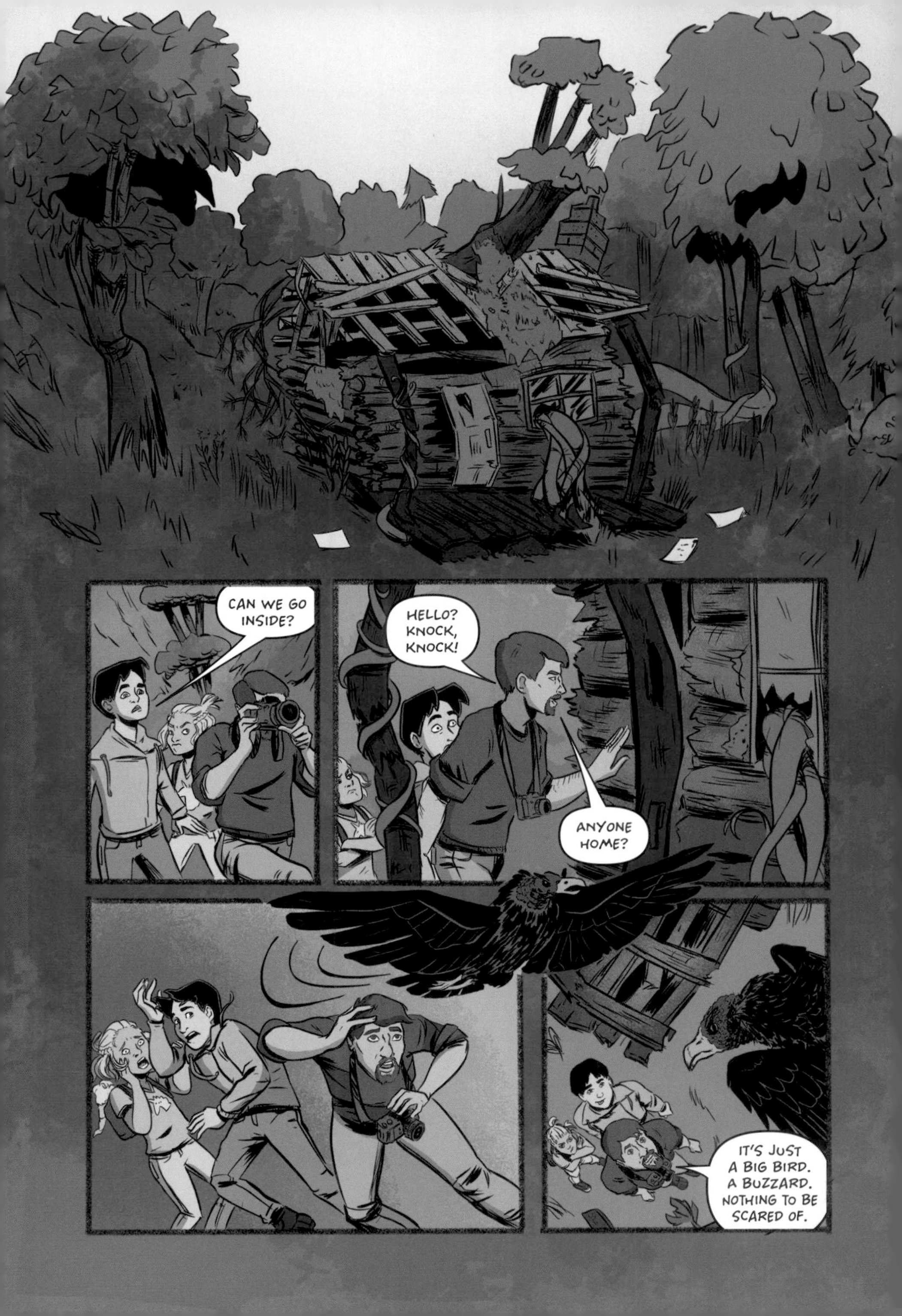
CAN WE GO INSIDE?
HELLO? KNOCK, KNOCK!
ANYONE HOME?
IT'S JUST A BIG BIRD. A BUZZARD. NOTHING TO BE SCARED OF.

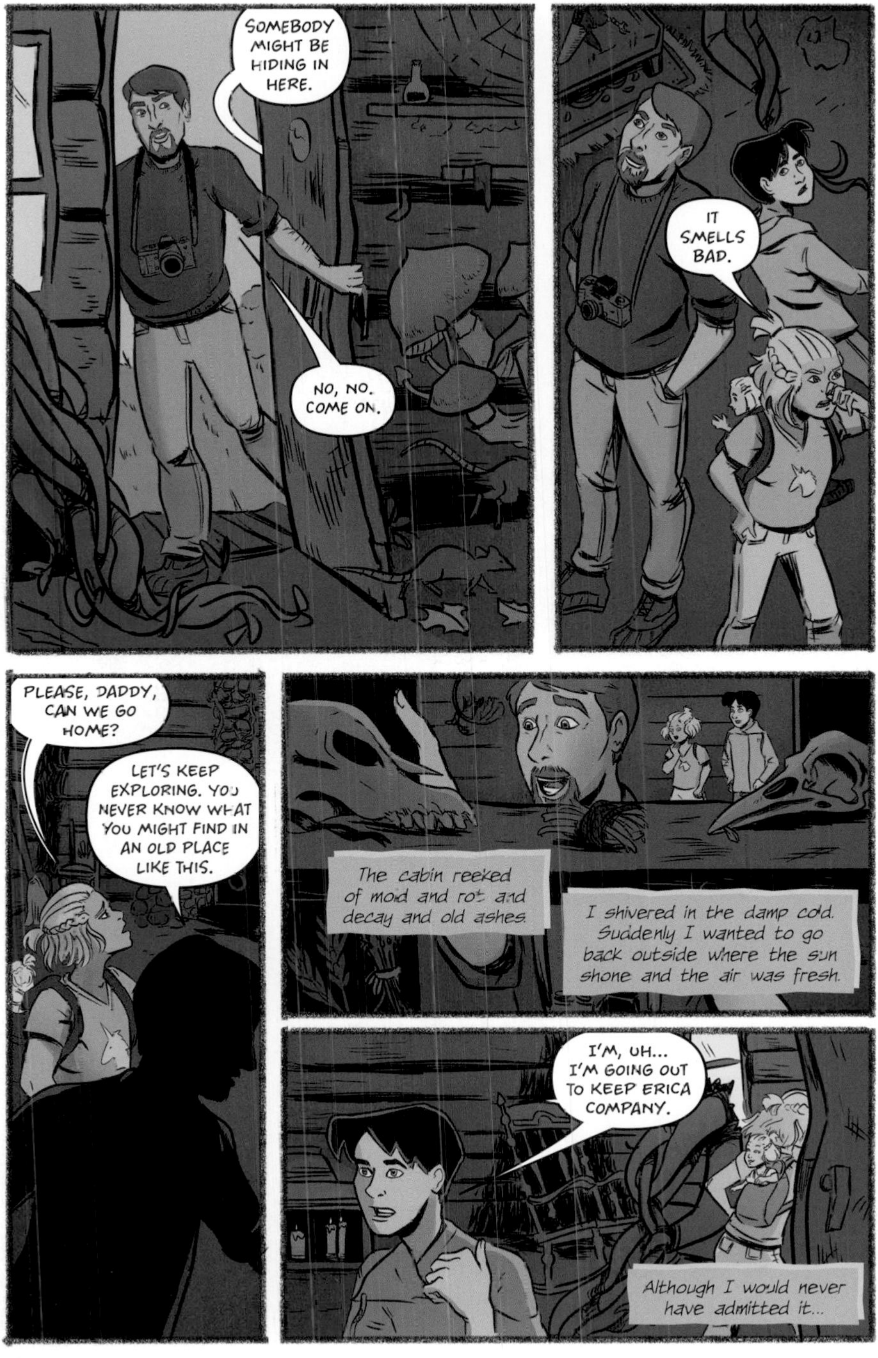
SOMEBODY MIGHT BE HIDING IN HERE.
NO, NO. COME ON.
IT SMELLS BAD.
PLEASE, DADDY, CAN WE GO HOME?
LET'S KEEP EXPLORING. YOU NEVER KNOW WHAT YOU MIGHT FIND IN AN OLD PLACE LIKE THIS.
The cabin reeked of mold and rot and decay and old ashes.
I shivered in the damp cold. Suddenly I wanted to go back outside where the sun shone and the air was fresh.
I'M, UH... I'M GOING OUT TO KEEP ERICA COMPANY.
Although I would never have admitted it...

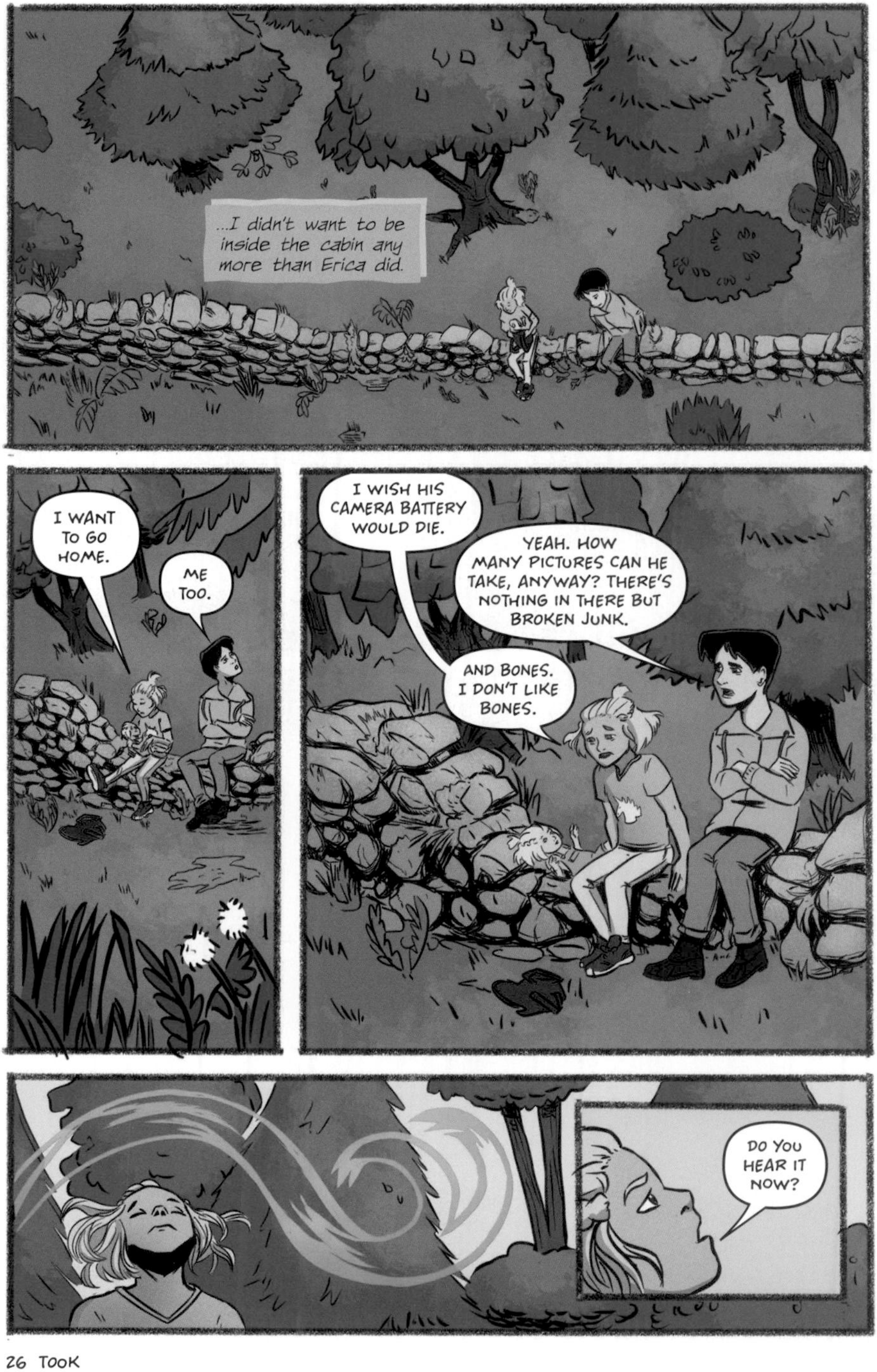
...I didn't want to be inside the cabin any more than Erica did.
I WANT TO GO HOME.
ME TOO.
I WISH HIS CAMERA BATTERY WOULD DIE.
YEAH. HOW MANY PICTURES CAN HE TAKE, ANYWAY? THERE'S NOTHING IN THERE BUT BROKEN JUNK.
AND BONES. I DON'T LIKE BONES.
DO YOU HEAR IT NOW?

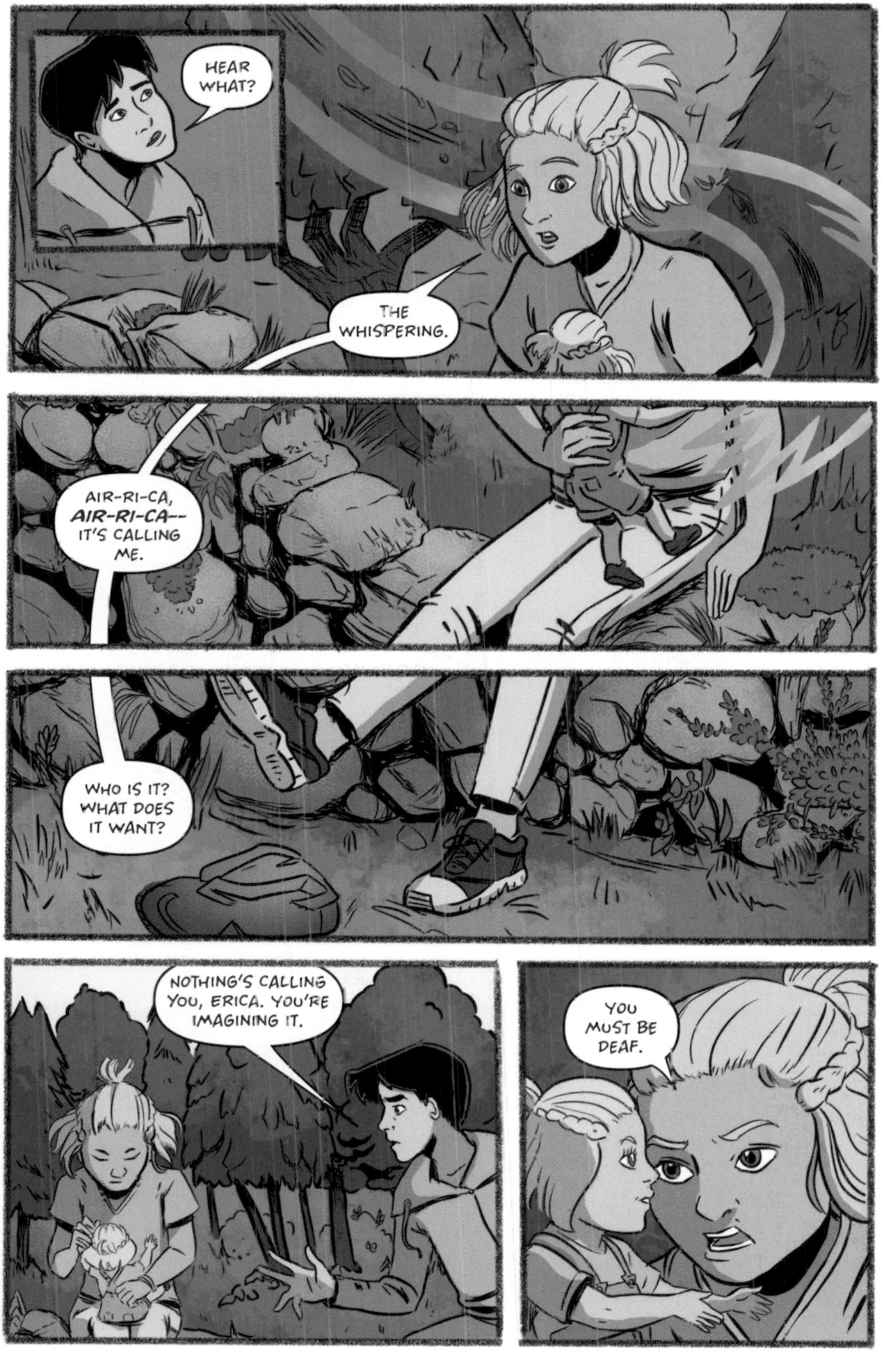
HEAR WHAT?
THE WHISPERING.
AIR-RI-CA, **AIR-RI-CA--** IT'S CALLING ME.
WHO IS IT? WHAT DOES IT WANT?
NOTHING'S CALLING YOU, ERICA. YOU'RE IMAGINING IT.
YOU MUST BE DEAF.

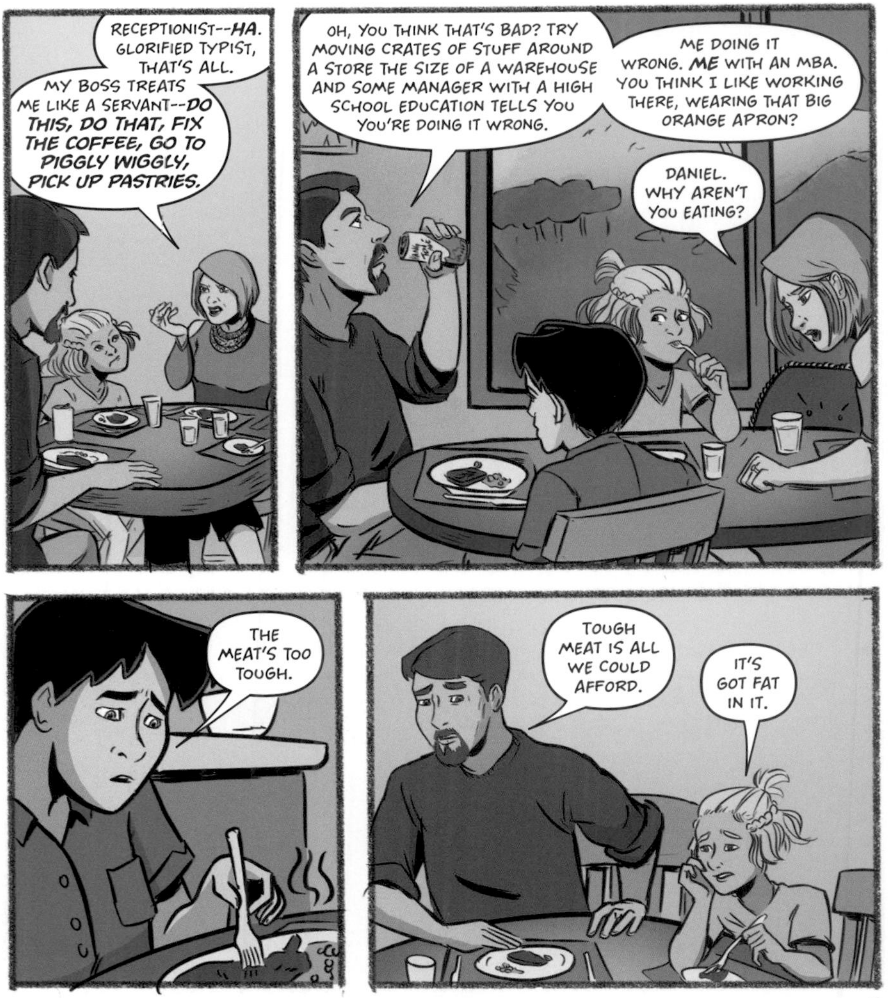
RECEPTIONIST--**HA.** GLORIFIED TYPIST, THAT'S ALL.
MY BOSS TREATS ME LIKE A SERVANT--***DO THIS, DO THAT, FIX THE COFFEE, GO TO PIGGLY WIGGLY, PICK UP PASTRIES.***
OH, YOU THINK THAT'S BAD? TRY MOVING CRATES OF STUFF AROUND A STORE THE SIZE OF A WAREHOUSE AND SOME MANAGER WITH A HIGH SCHOOL EDUCATION TELLS YOU YOU'RE DOING IT WRONG.
ME DOING IT WRONG. ***ME*** WITH AN MBA. YOU THINK I LIKE WORKING THERE, WEARING THAT BIG ORANGE APRON?
DANIEL. WHY AREN'T YOU EATING?
THE MEAT'S TOO TOUGH.
TOUGH MEAT IS ALL WE COULD AFFORD.
IT'S GOT FAT IN IT.
WELL, THEN DON'T EAT.
WHERE ARE YOU GOING, TED? YOU HAVEN'T FINISHED YOUR DINNER.
I'M AN ADULT. I DON'T NEED PERMISSION TO LEAVE THE TABLE.

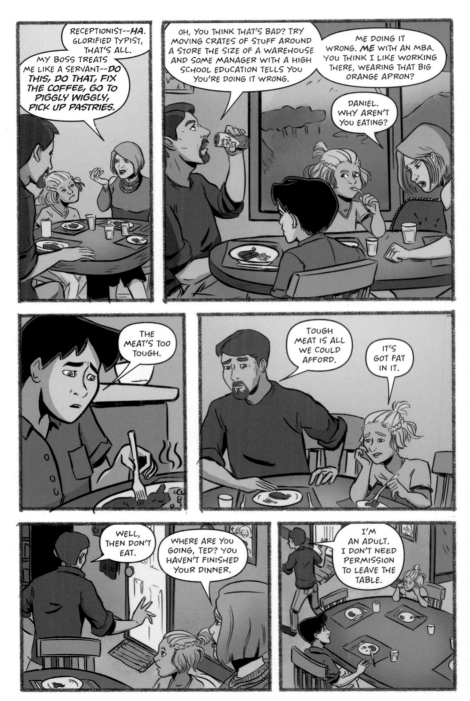

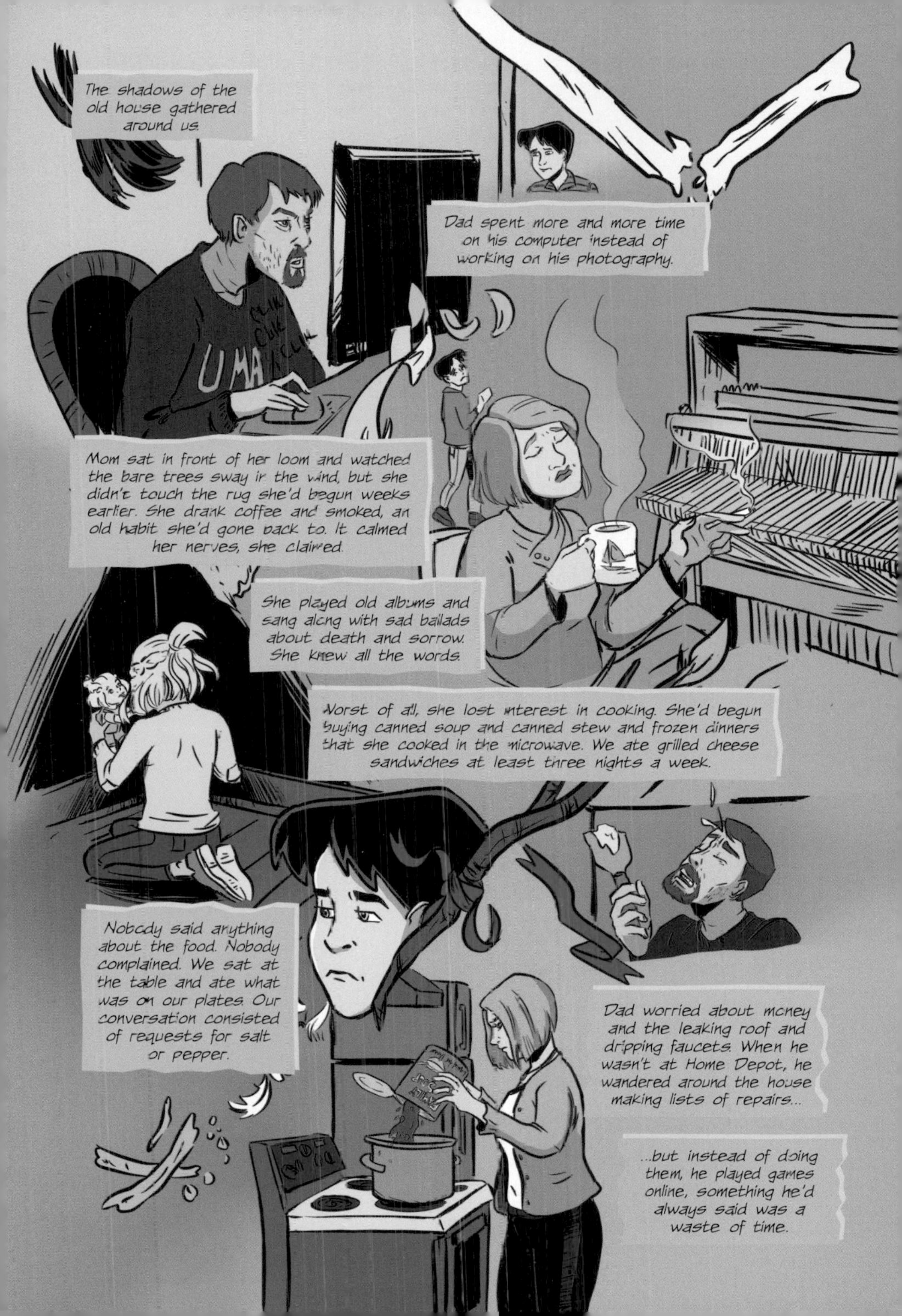
The shadows of the old house gathered around us.
Dad spent more and more time on his computer instead of working on his photography.
Mom sat in front of her loom and watched the bare trees sway in the wind, but she didn't touch the rug she'd begun weeks earlier. She drank coffee and smoked, an old habit she'd gone back to. It calmed her nerves, she claimed.
She played old albums and sang along with sad ballads about death and sorrow. She knew all the words.
Worst of all, she lost interest in cooking. She'd begun buying canned soup and canned stew and frozen dinners that she cooked in the microwave. We ate grilled cheese sandwiches at least three nights a week.
Nobody said anything about the food. Nobody complained. We sat at the table and ate what was on our plates. Our conversation consisted of requests for salt or pepper.
Dad worried about money and the leaking roof and dripping faucets. When he wasn't at Home Depot, he wandered around the house making lists of repairs...
...but instead of doing them, he played games online, something he'd always said was a waste of time.

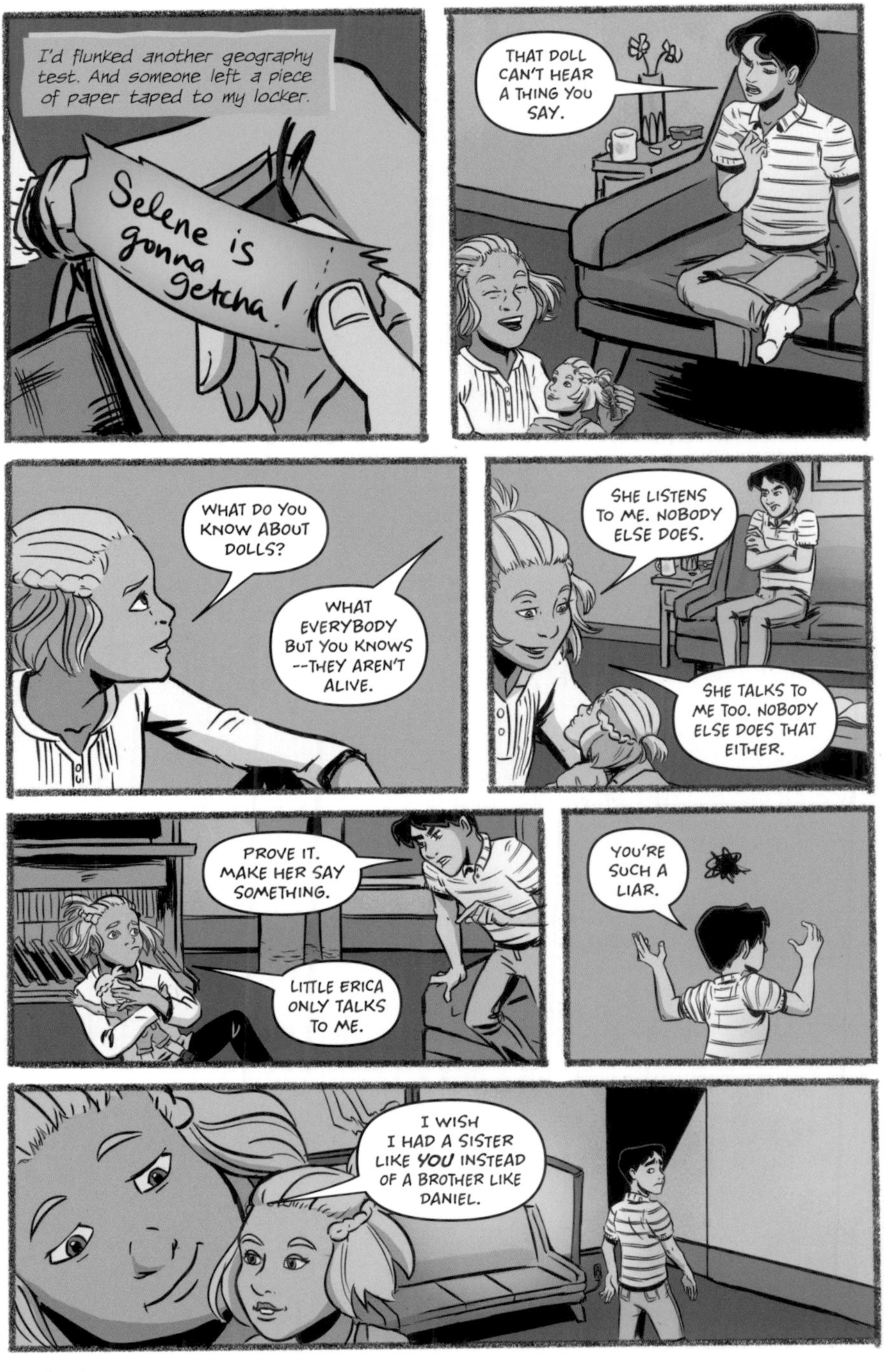
I'd flunked another geography test. And someone left a piece of paper taped to my locker.
Selene is gonna getcha!
THAT DOLL CAN'T HEAR A THING YOU SAY.
WHAT DO YOU KNOW ABOUT DOLLS?
WHAT EVERYBODY BUT YOU KNOWS --THEY AREN'T ALIVE.
SHE LISTENS TO ME. NOBODY ELSE DOES.
SHE TALKS TO ME TOO. NOBODY ELSE DOES THAT EITHER.
PROVE IT. MAKE HER SAY SOMETHING.
LITTLE ERICA ONLY TALKS TO ME.
YOU'RE SUCH A LIAR.
I WISH I HAD A SISTER LIKE ***YOU*** INSTEAD OF A BROTHER LIKE DANIEL.

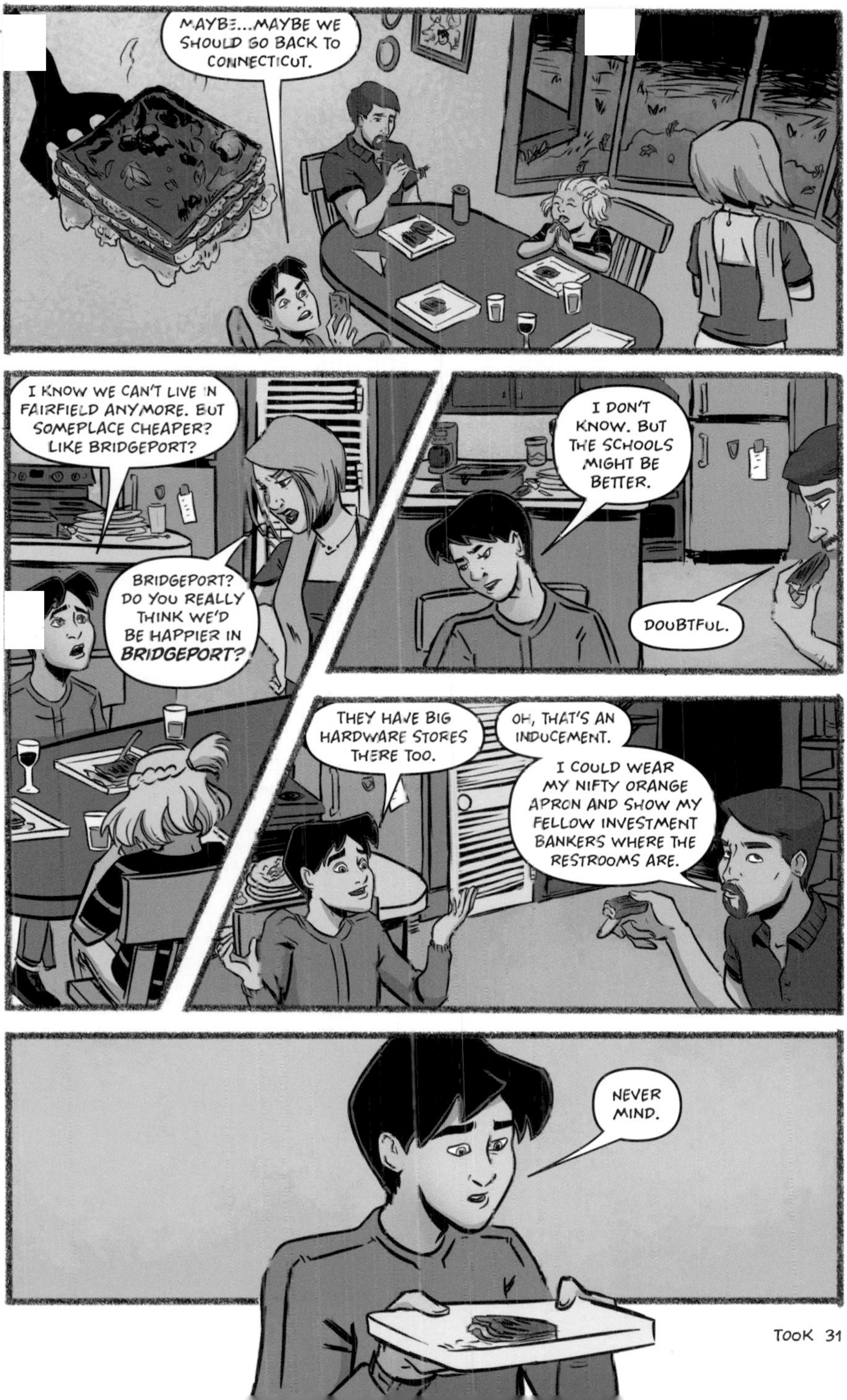
MAYBE...MAYBE WE SHOULD GO BACK TO CONNECTICUT.
I KNOW WE CAN'T LIVE IN FAIRFIELD ANYMORE. BUT SOMEPLACE CHEAPER? LIKE BRIDGEPORT?
BRIDGEPORT? DO YOU REALLY THINK WE'D BE HAPPIER IN BRIDGEPORT?
I DON'T KNOW. BUT THE SCHOOLS MIGHT BE BETTER.
DOUBTFUL.
THEY HAVE BIG HARDWARE STORES THERE TOO.
OH, THAT'S AN INDUCEMENT.
I COULD WEAR MY NIFTY ORANGE APRON AND SHOW MY FELLOW INVESTMENT BANKERS WHERE THE RESTROOMS ARE.
NEVER MIND.

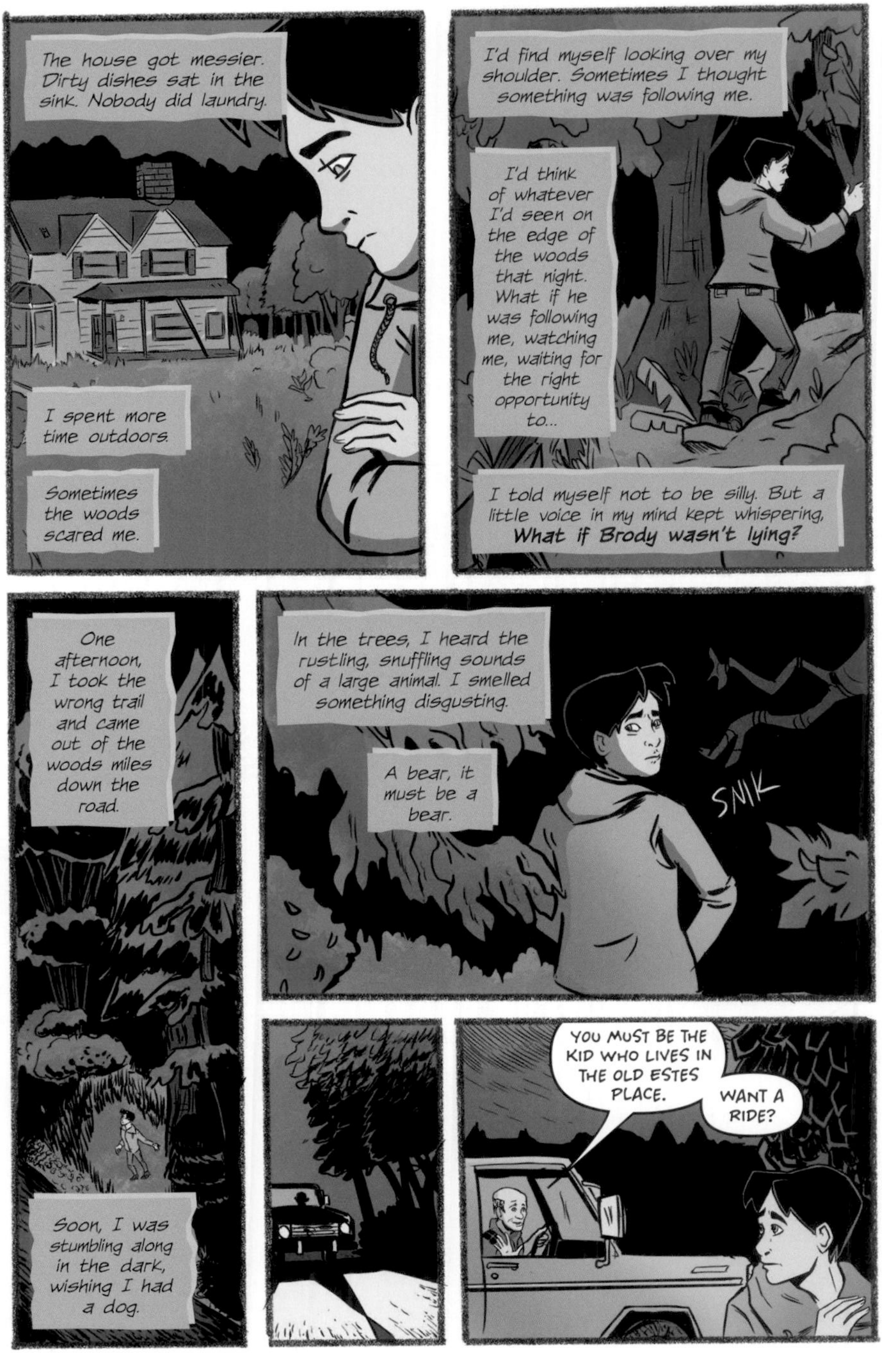

The house got messier. Dirty dishes sat in the sink. Nobody did laundry.
I spent more time outdoors.
Sometimes the woods scared me.
I'd find myself looking over my shoulder. Sometimes I thought something was following me.
I'd think of whatever I'd seen on the edge of the woods that night. What if he was following me, watching me, waiting for the right opportunity to...
I told myself not to be silly. But a little voice in my mind kept whispering, **What if Brody wasn't lying?**
One afternoon, I took the wrong trail and came out of the woods miles down the road.
Soon, I was stumbling along in the dark, wishing I had a dog.
In the trees, I heard the rustling, snuffling sounds of a large animal. I smelled something disgusting.
A bear, it must be a bear.
SNIK
YOU MUST BE THE KID WHO LIVES IN THE OLD ESTES PLACE.
WANT A RIDE?

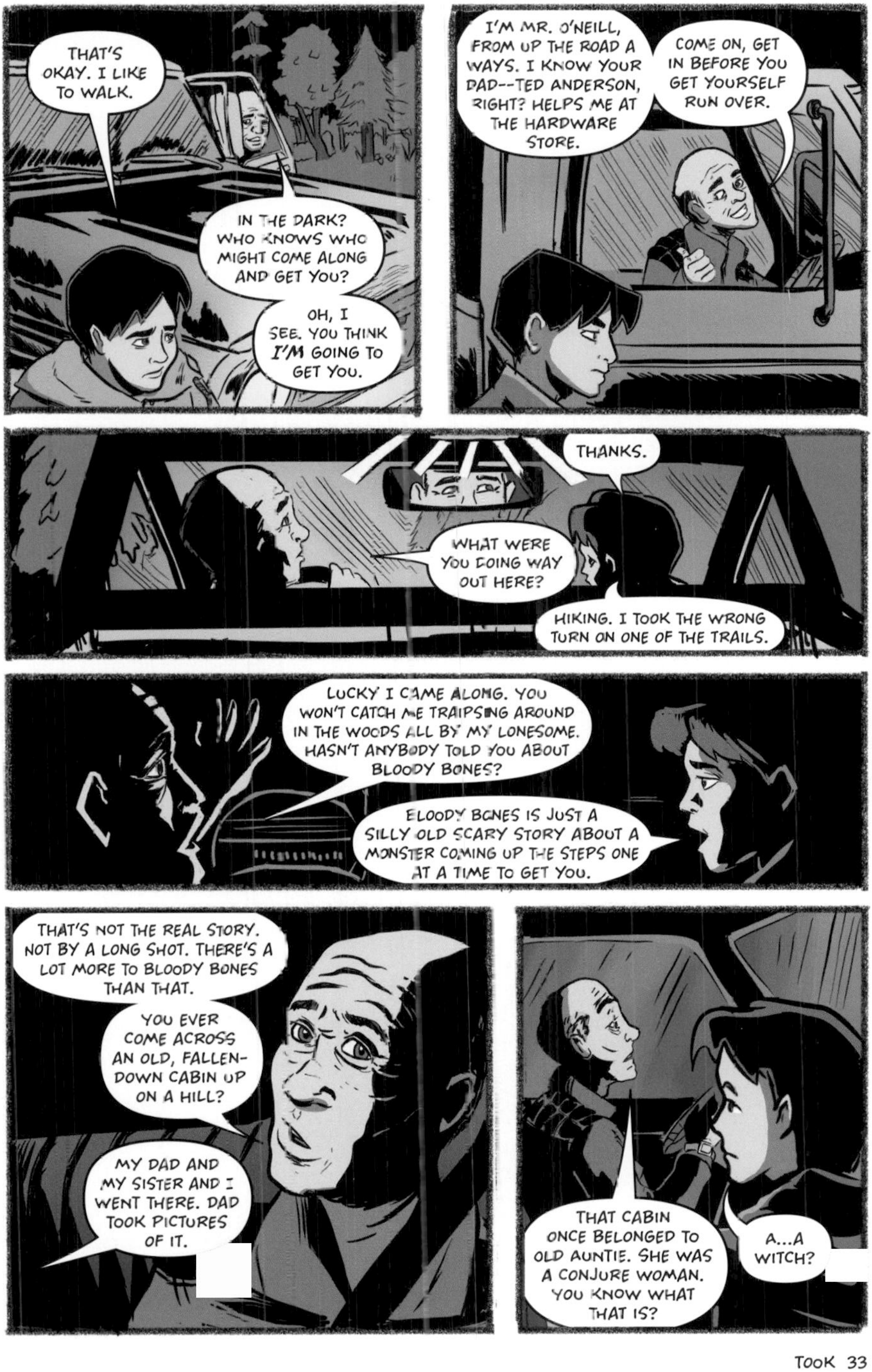
THAT'S OKAY. I LIKE TO WALK.
IN THE DARK? WHO KNOWS WHO MIGHT COME ALONG AND GET YOU?
OH, I SEE. YOU THINK *I'M* GOING TO GET YOU.
I'M MR. O'NEILL, FROM UP THE ROAD A WAYS. I KNOW YOUR DAD--TED ANDERSON, RIGHT? HELPS ME AT THE HARDWARE STORE.
COME ON, GET IN BEFORE YOU GET YOURSELF RUN OVER.
THANKS.
WHAT WERE YOU DOING WAY OUT HERE?
HIKING. I TOOK THE WRONG TURN ON ONE OF THE TRAILS.
LUCKY I CAME ALONG. YOU WON'T CATCH ME TRAIPSING AROUND IN THE WOODS ALL BY MY LONESOME. HASN'T ANYBODY TOLD YOU ABOUT BLOODY BONES?
BLOODY BONES IS JUST A SILLY OLD SCARY STORY ABOUT A MONSTER COMING UP THE STEPS ONE AT A TIME TO GET YOU.
THAT'S NOT THE REAL STORY. NOT BY A LONG SHOT. THERE'S A LOT MORE TO BLOODY BONES THAN THAT.
YOU EVER COME ACROSS AN OLD, FALLEN-DOWN CABIN UP ON A HILL?
MY DAD AND MY SISTER AND I WENT THERE. DAD TOOK PICTURES OF IT.
THAT CABIN ONCE BELONGED TO OLD AUNTIE. SHE WAS A CONJURE WOMAN. YOU KNOW WHAT THAT IS?
A...A WITCH?

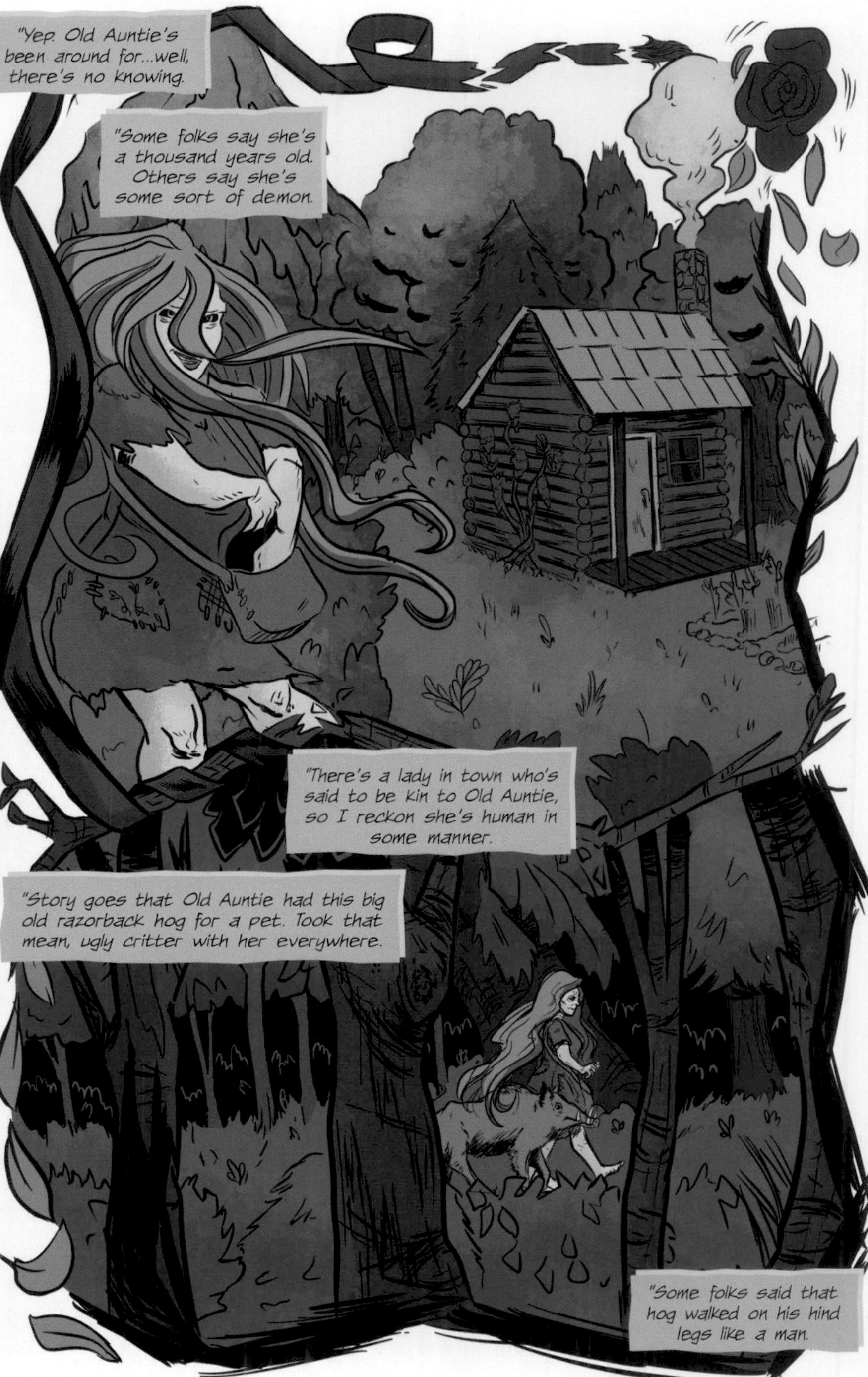
"Yep. Old Auntie's been around for...well, there's no knowing.
"Some folks say she's a thousand years old. Others say she's some sort of demon.
"There's a lady in town who's said to be kin to Old Auntie, so I reckon she's human in some manner.
"Story goes that Old Auntie had this big old razorback hog for a pet. Took that mean, ugly critter with her everywhere.
"Some folks said that hog walked on his hind legs like a man.

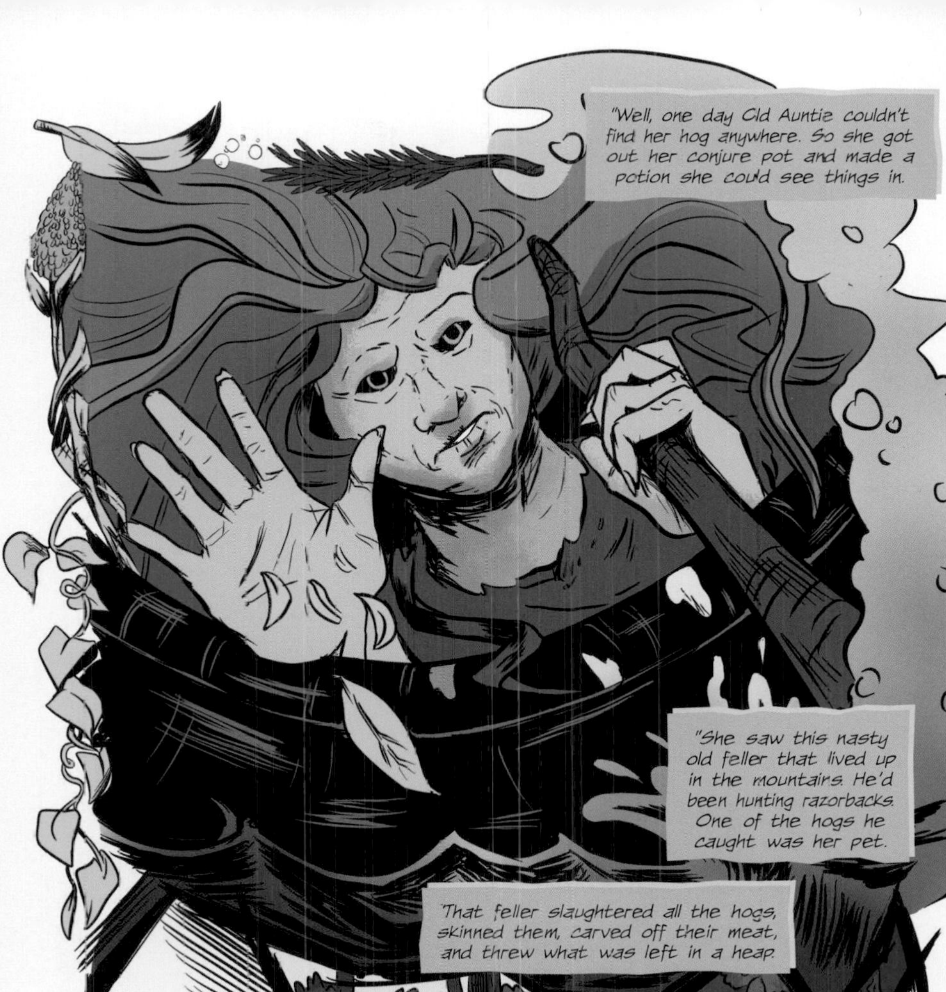
"Well, one day Old Auntie couldn't find her hog anywhere. So she got out her conjure pot and made a potion she could see things in.
"She saw this nasty old feller that lived up in the mountains. He'd been hunting razorbacks. One of the hogs he caught was her pet.
"That feller slaughtered all the hogs, skinned them, carved off their meat, and threw what was left in a heap.
"In that pile, Old Auntie saw her hog's bald head and bloody bones.
"So she cast a spell to summon him back from the dead.

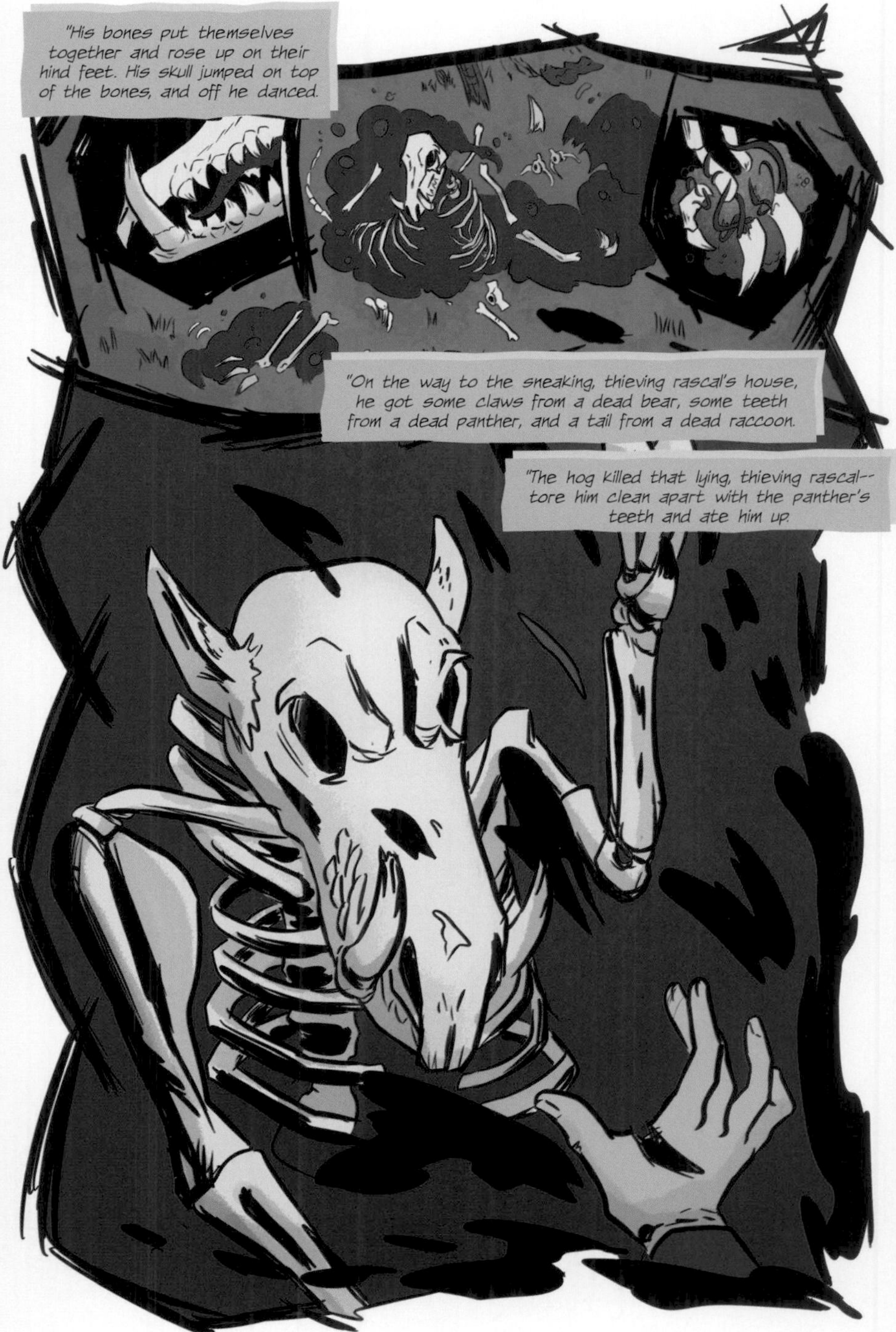
"His bones put themselves together and rose up on their hind feet. His skull jumped on top of the bones, and off he danced.
"On the way to the sneaking, thieving rascal's house, he got some claws from a dead bear, some teeth from a dead panther, and a tail from a dead raccoon.
"The hog killed that lying, thieving rascal--tore him clean apart with the panther's teeth and ate him up.

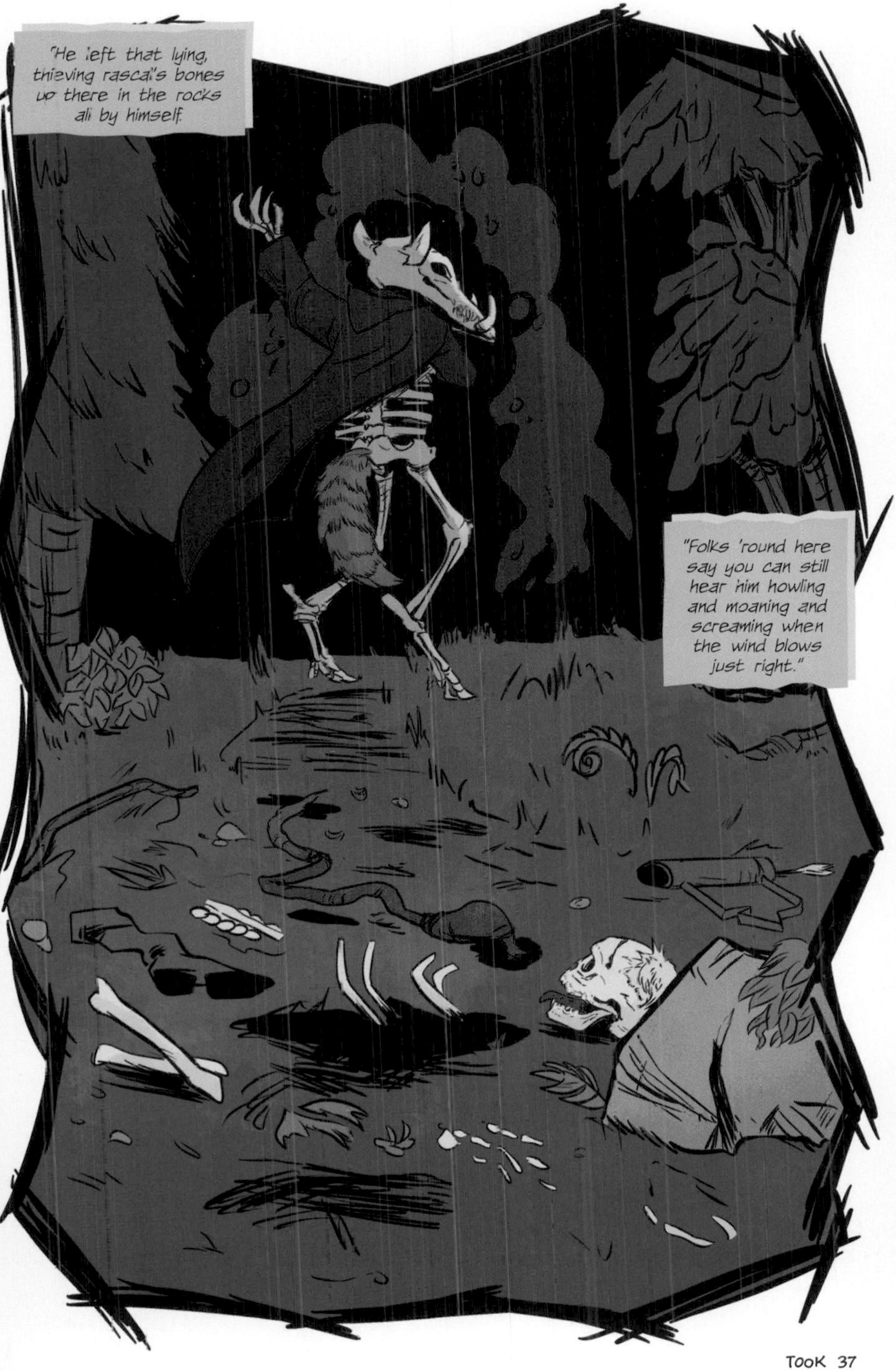
"He left that lying, thieving rascal's bones up there in the rocks all by himself.
"Folks 'round here say you can still hear him howling and moaning and screaming when the wind blows just right."

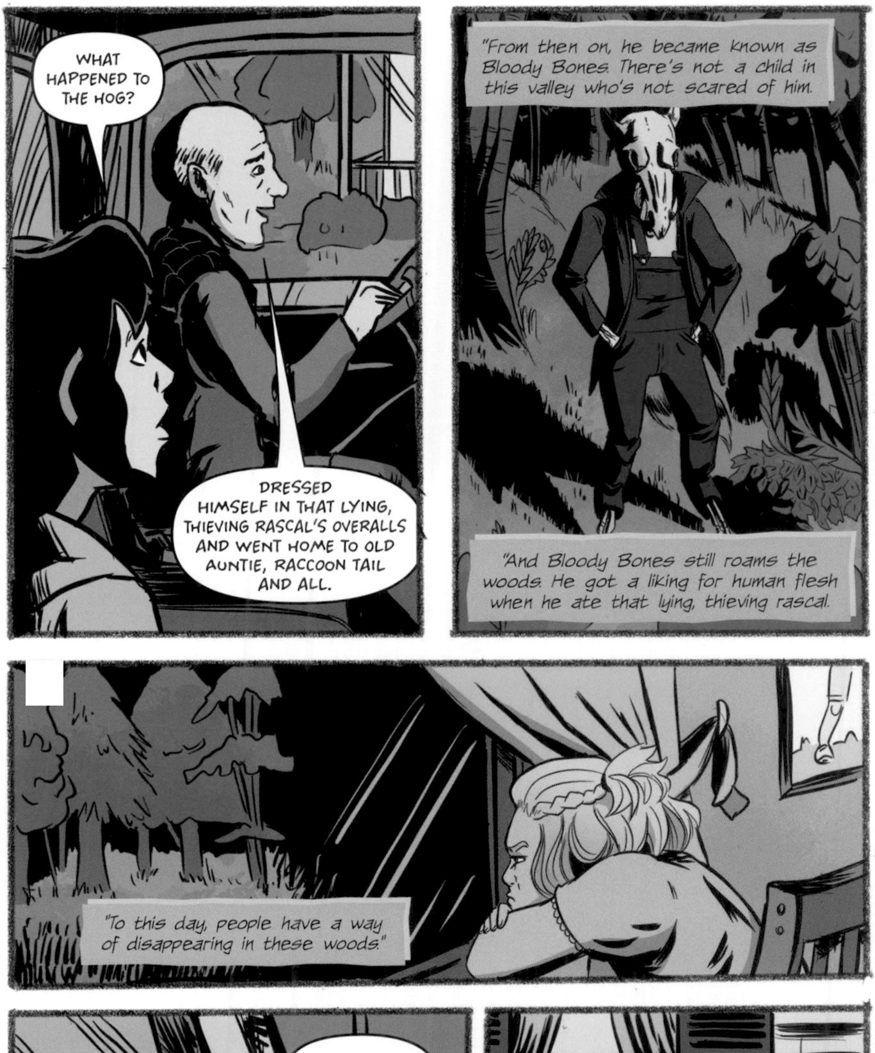
WHAT HAPPENED TO THE HOG?
DRESSED HIMSELF IN THAT LYING, THIEVING RASCAL'S OVERALLS AND WENT HOME TO OLD AUNTIE, RACCOON TAIL AND ALL.
"From then on, he became known as Bloody Bones. There's not a child in this valley who's not scared of him.
"And Bloody Bones still roams the woods. He got a liking for human flesh when he ate that lying, thieving rascal.
"To this day, people have a way of disappearing in these woods."
THAT YOUR LITTLE SISTER? SHE'S A PRETTY LITTLE THING.
TAKE GOOD CARE OF HER, SON. DON'T LET HER GO WANDERING OFF LIKE...
LIKE SELENE?

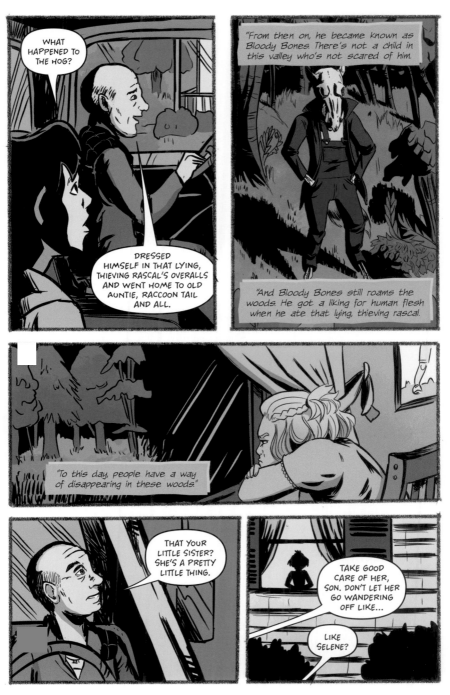

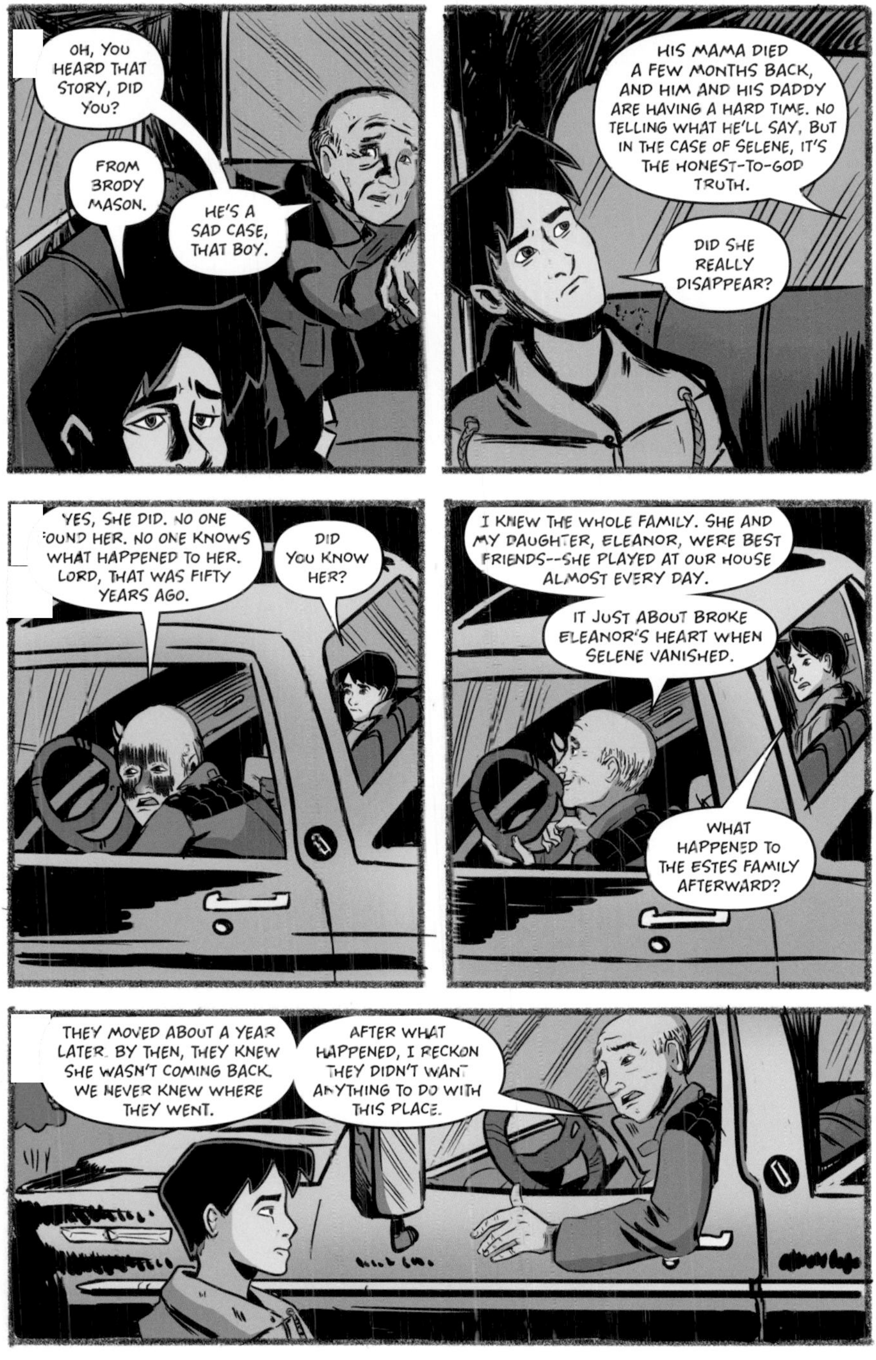

OH, YOU HEARD THAT STORY, DID YOU?
FROM BRODY MASON.
HE'S A SAD CASE, THAT BOY.
HIS MAMA DIED A FEW MONTHS BACK, AND HIM AND HIS DADDY ARE HAVING A HARD TIME. NO TELLING WHAT HE'LL SAY, BUT IN THE CASE OF SELENE, IT'S THE HONEST-TO-GOD TRUTH.
DID SHE REALLY DISAPPEAR?
YES, SHE DID. NO ONE FOUND HER. NO ONE KNOWS WHAT HAPPENED TO HER. LORD, THAT WAS FIFTY YEARS AGO.
DID YOU KNOW HER?
I KNEW THE WHOLE FAMILY. SHE AND MY DAUGHTER, ELEANOR, WERE BEST FRIENDS--SHE PLAYED AT OUR HOUSE ALMOST EVERY DAY.
IT JUST ABOUT BROKE ELEANOR'S HEART WHEN SELENE VANISHED.
WHAT HAPPENED TO THE ESTES FAMILY AFTERWARD?
THEY MOVED ABOUT A YEAR LATER. BY THEN, THEY KNEW SHE WASN'T COMING BACK. WE NEVER KNEW WHERE THEY WENT.
AFTER WHAT HAPPENED, I RECKON THEY DIDN'T WANT ANYTHING TO DO WITH THIS PLACE.

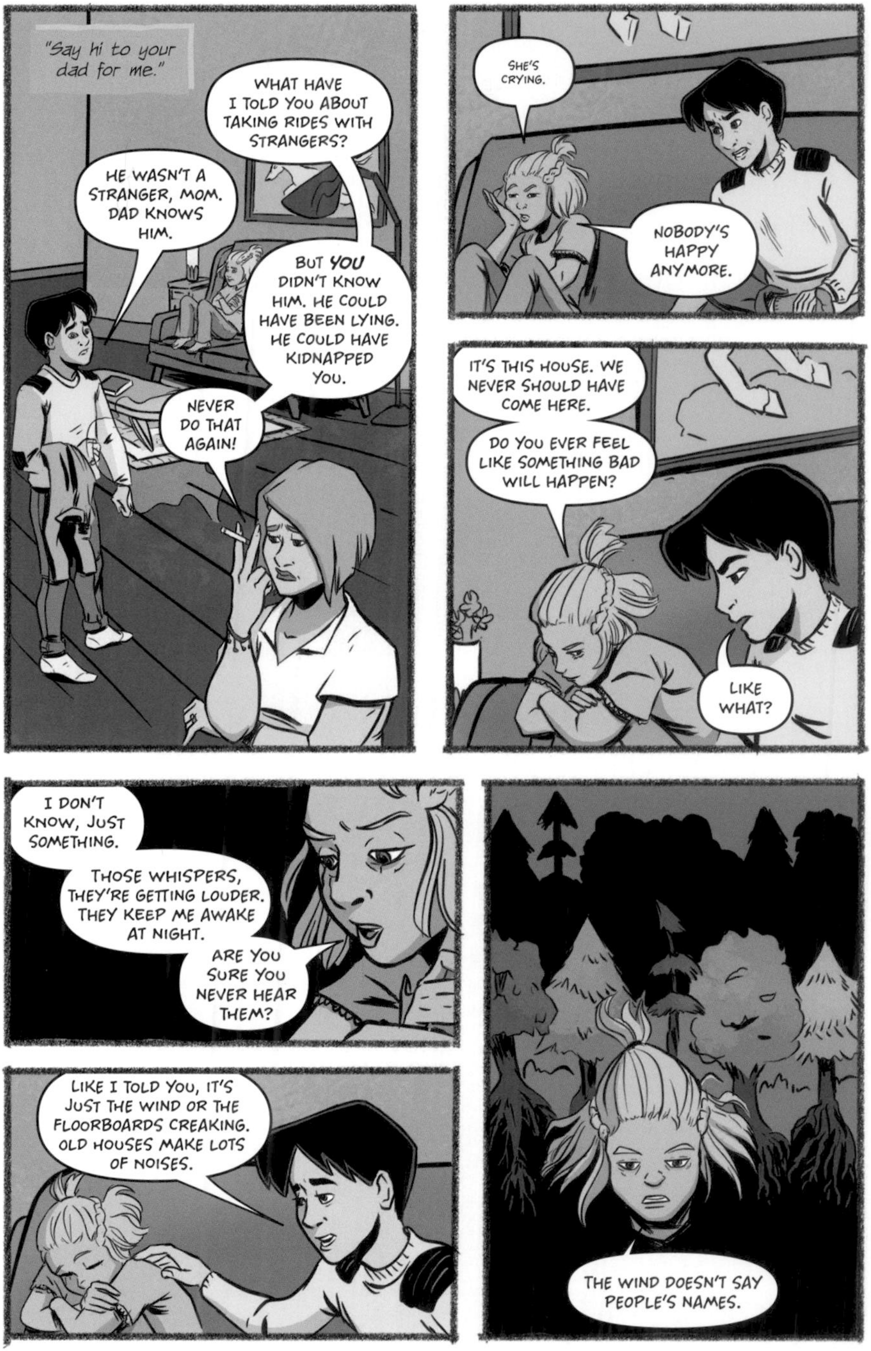
"Say hi to your dad for me."
WHAT HAVE I TOLD YOU ABOUT TAKING RIDES WITH STRANGERS?
HE WASN'T A STRANGER, MOM. DAD KNOWS HIM.
BUT YOU DIDN'T KNOW HIM. HE COULD HAVE BEEN LYING. HE COULD HAVE KIDNAPPED YOU.
NEVER DO THAT AGAIN!
SHE'S CRYING.
NOBODY'S HAPPY ANYMORE.
IT'S THIS HOUSE. WE NEVER SHOULD HAVE COME HERE.
DO YOU EVER FEEL LIKE SOMETHING BAD WILL HAPPEN?
LIKE WHAT?
I DON'T KNOW, JUST SOMETHING.
THOSE WHISPERS, THEY'RE GETTING LOUDER. THEY KEEP ME AWAKE AT NIGHT.
ARE YOU SURE YOU NEVER HEAR THEM?
LIKE I TOLD YOU, IT'S JUST THE WIND OR THE FLOORBOARDS CREAKING. OLD HOUSES MAKE LOTS OF NOISES.
THE WIND DOESN'T SAY PEOPLE'S NAMES.

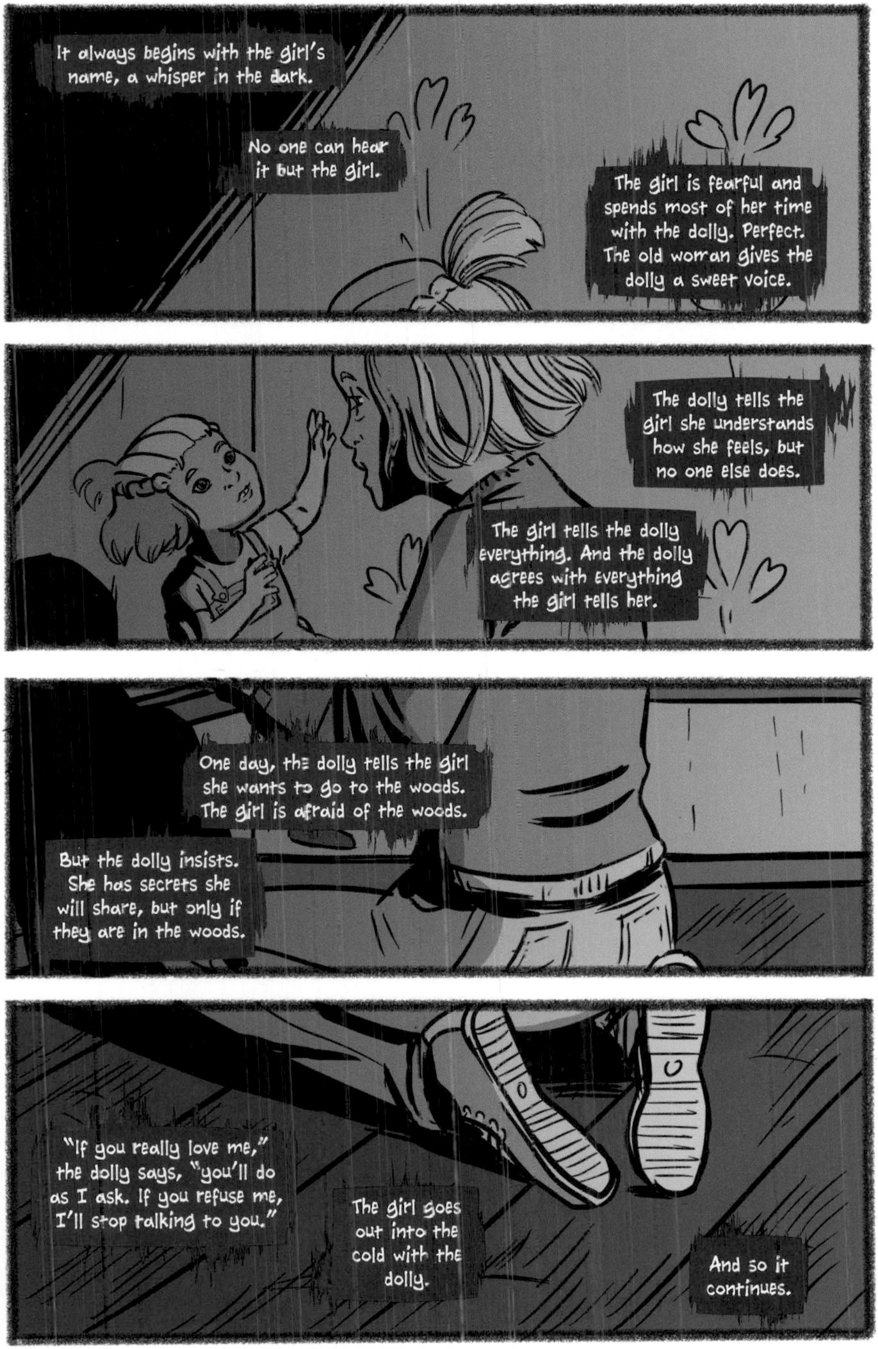
It always begins with the girl's name, a whisper in the dark.
No one can hear it but the girl.
The girl is fearful and spends most of her time with the dolly. Perfect. The old woman gives the dolly a sweet voice.
The dolly tells the girl she understands how she feels, but no one else does.
The girl tells the dolly everything. And the dolly agrees with everything the girl tells her.
One day, the dolly tells the girl she wants to go to the woods. The girl is afraid of the woods.
But the dolly insists. She has secrets she will share, but only if they are in the woods.
"If you really love me," the dolly says, "you'll do as I ask. If you refuse me, I'll stop talking to you."
The girl goes out into the cold with the dolly.
And so it continues.

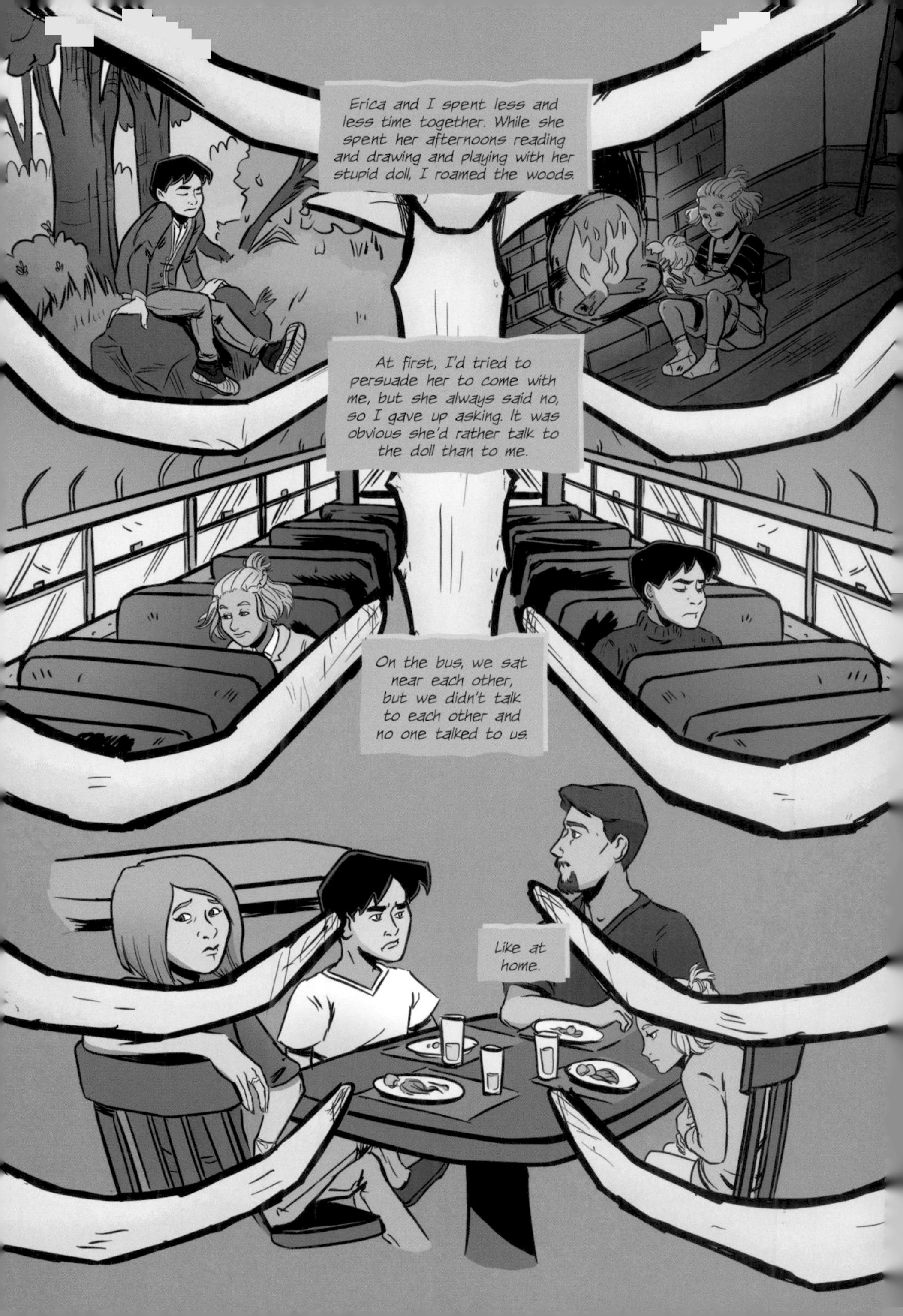
Erica and I spent less and less time together. While she spent her afternoons reading and drawing and playing with her stupid doll, I roamed the woods.
At first, I'd tried to persuade her to come with me, but she always said no, so I gave up asking. It was obvious she'd rather talk to the doll than to me.
On the bus, we sat near each other, but we didn't talk to each other and no one talked to us.
Like at home.

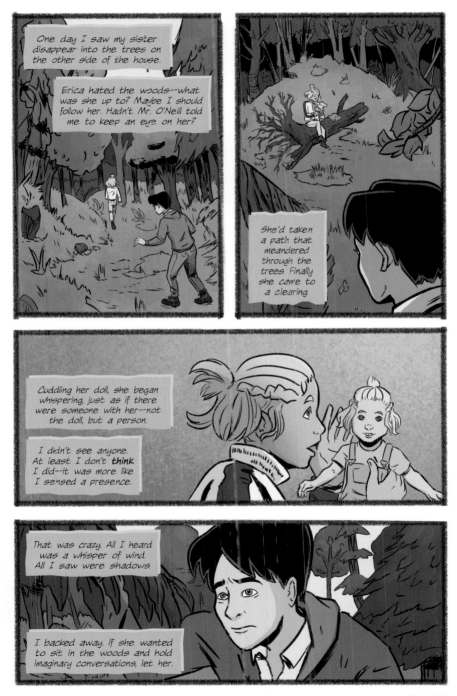

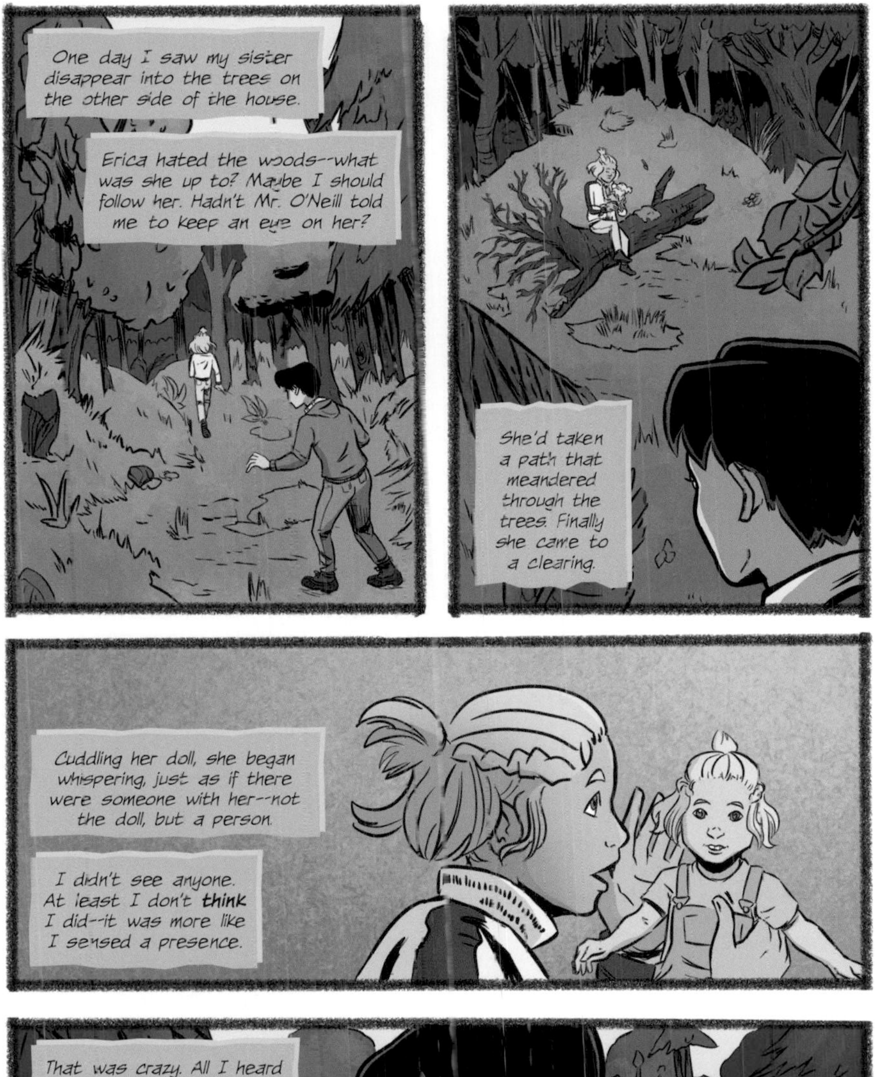
One day I saw my sister disappear into the trees on the other side of the house.
Erica hated the woods--what was she up to? Maybe I should follow her. Hadn't Mr. O'Neill told me to keep an eye on her?
She'd taken a path that meandered through the trees. Finally she came to a clearing.
Cuddling her doll, she began whispering, just as if there were someone with her--not the doll, but a person.
I didn't see anyone. At least I don't **think** I did--it was more like I sensed a presence.
That was crazy. All I heard was a whisper of wind. All I saw were shadows.
I backed away. If she wanted to sit in the woods and hold imaginary conversations, let her.

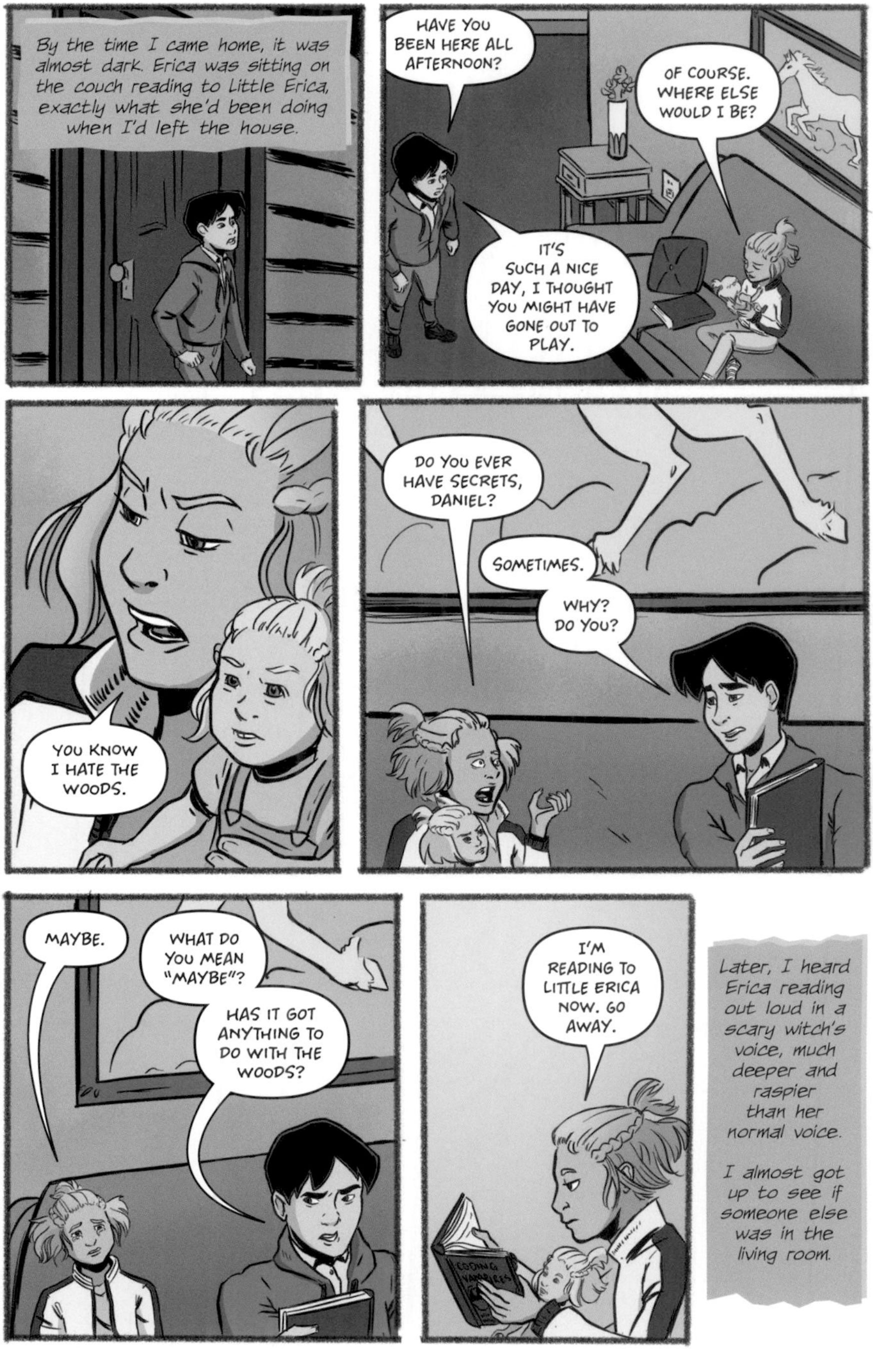
By the time I came home, it was almost dark. Erica was sitting on the couch reading to Little Erica, exactly what she'd been doing when I'd left the house.
HAVE YOU BEEN HERE ALL AFTERNOON?
OF COURSE. WHERE ELSE WOULD I BE?
IT'S SUCH A NICE DAY, I THOUGHT YOU MIGHT HAVE GONE OUT TO PLAY.
YOU KNOW I HATE THE WOODS.
DO YOU EVER HAVE SECRETS, DANIEL?
SOMETIMES.
WHY? DO YOU?
MAYBE.
WHAT DO YOU MEAN "MAYBE"?
HAS IT GOT ANYTHING TO DO WITH THE WOODS?
I'M READING TO LITTLE ERICA NOW. GO AWAY.
Later, I heard Erica reading out loud in a scary witch's voice, much deeper and raspier than her normal voice.
I almost got up to see if someone else was in the living room.

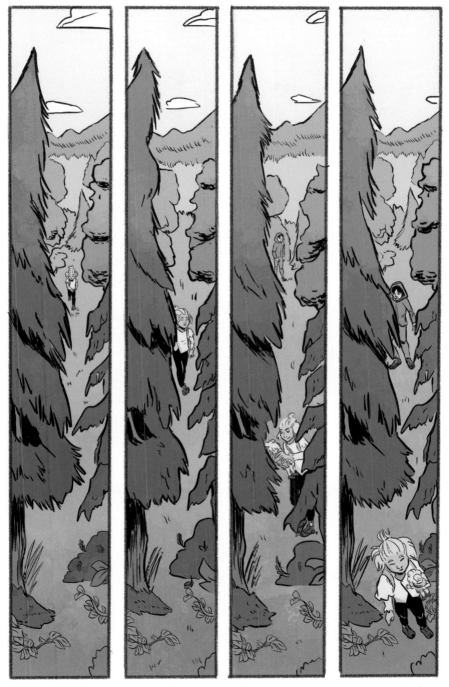

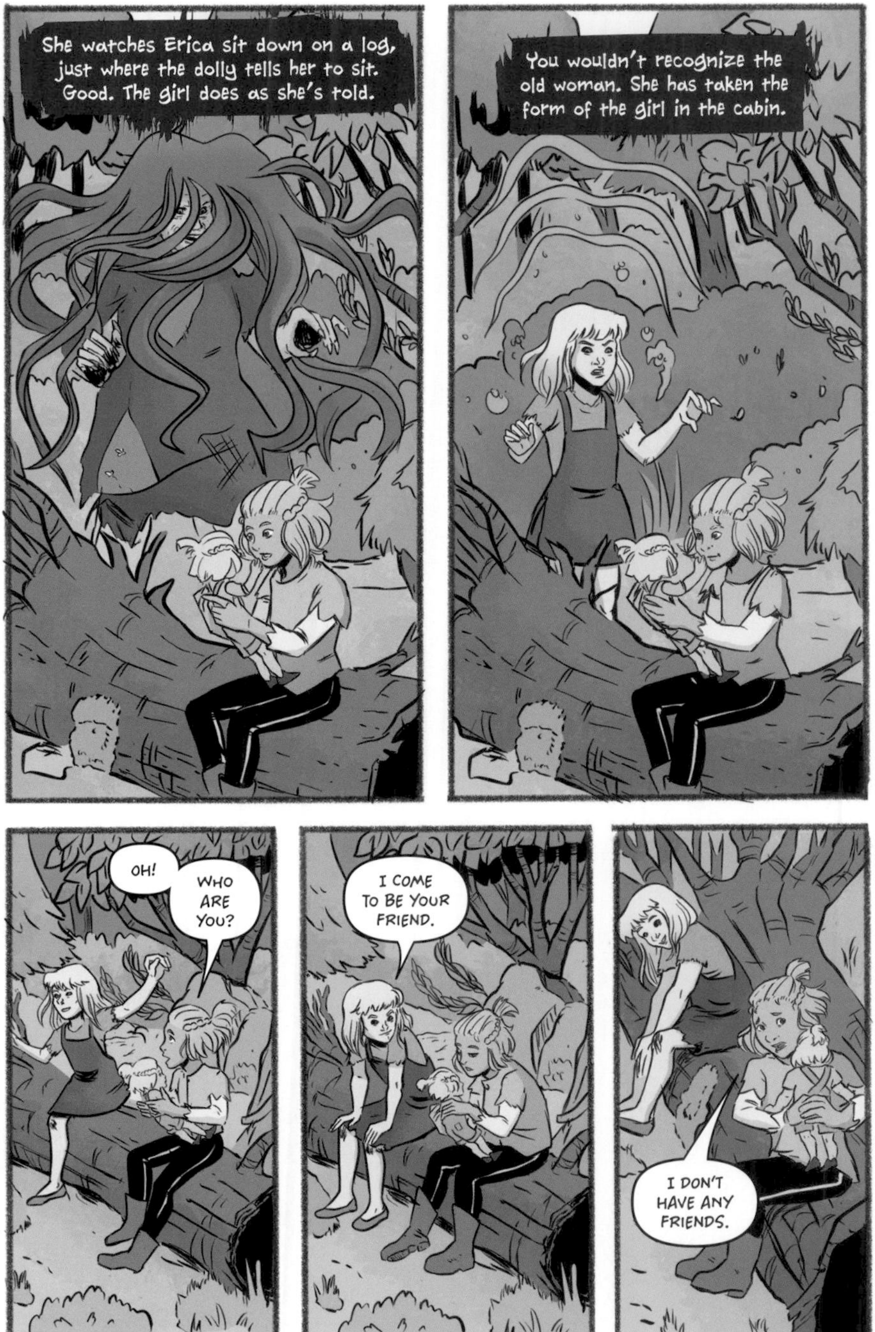
She watches Erica sit down on a log, just where the dolly tells her to sit. Good. The girl does as she's told.
You wouldn't recognize the old woman. She has taken the form of the girl in the cabin.
OH!
WHO ARE YOU?
I COME TO BE YOUR FRIEND.
I DON'T HAVE ANY FRIENDS.

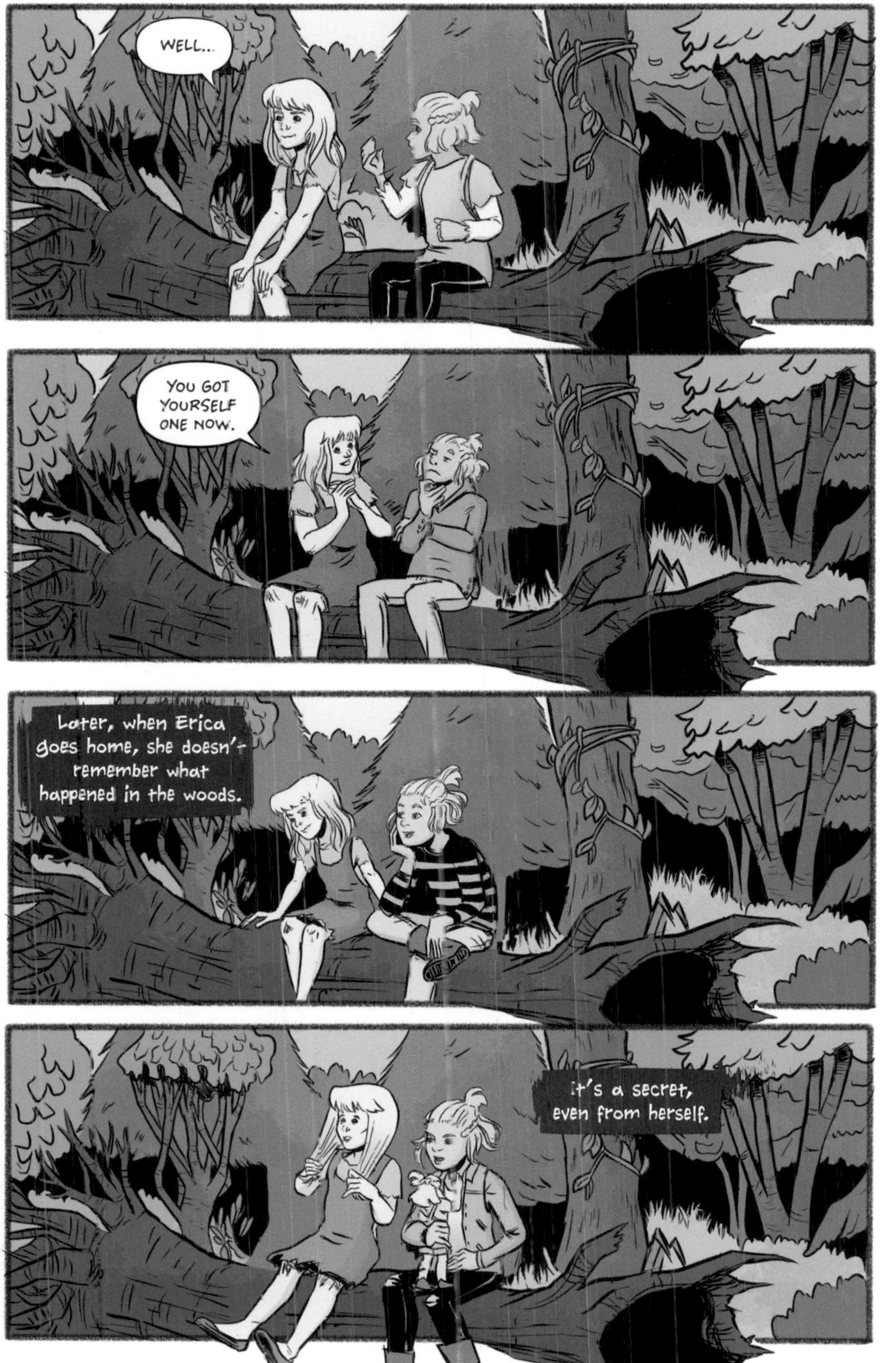
WELL...
YOU GOT YOURSELF ONE NOW.
Later, when Erica goes home, she doesn't remember what happened in the woods.
It's a secret, even from herself.

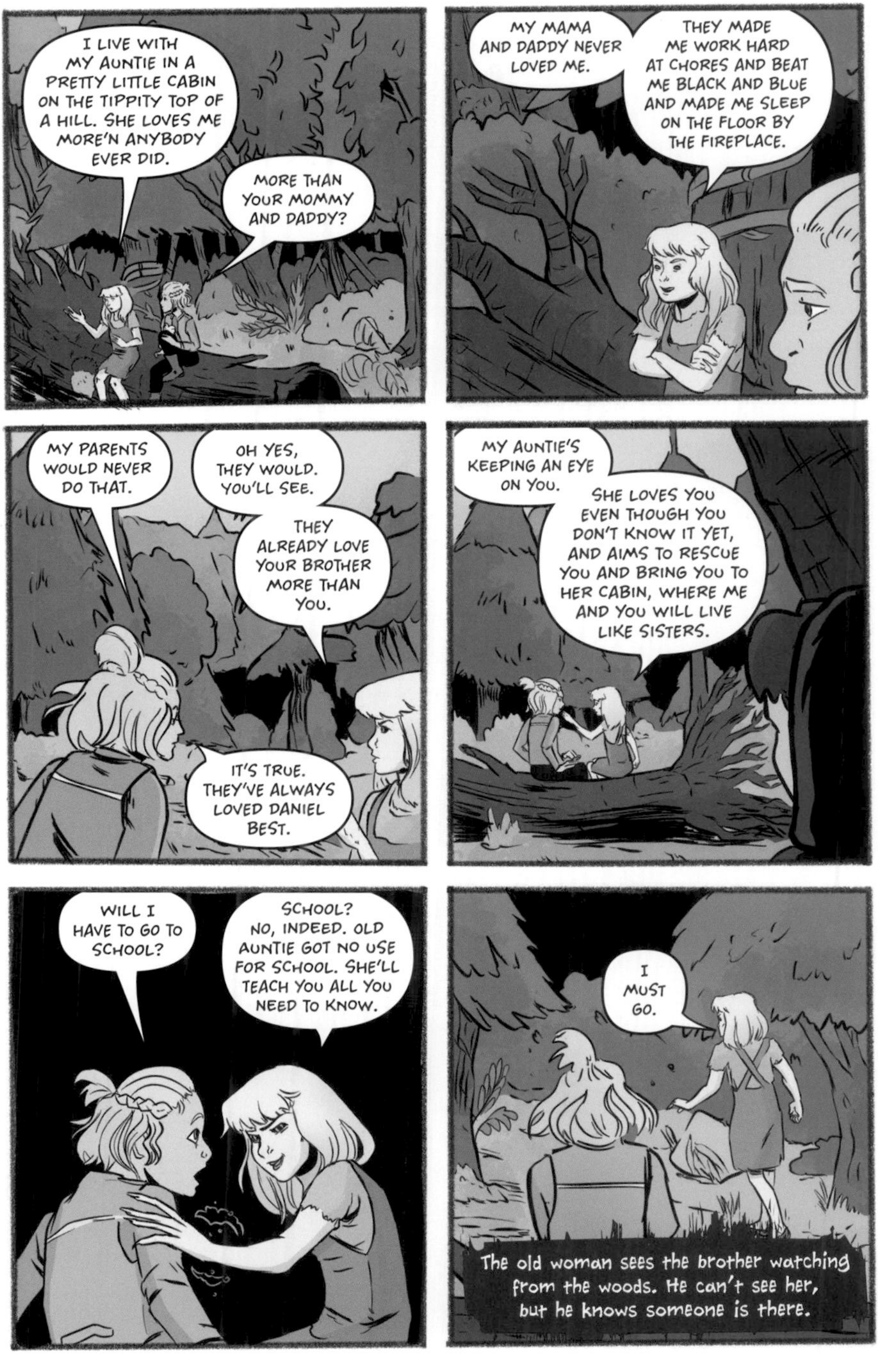
I LIVE WITH MY AUNTIE IN A PRETTY LITTLE CABIN ON THE TIPPITY TOP OF A HILL. SHE LOVES ME MORE'N ANYBODY EVER DID.
MORE THAN YOUR MOMMY AND DADDY?
MY MAMA AND DADDY NEVER LOVED ME.
THEY MADE ME WORK HARD AT CHORES AND BEAT ME BLACK AND BLUE AND MADE ME SLEEP ON THE FLOOR BY THE FIREPLACE.
MY PARENTS WOULD NEVER DO THAT.
OH YES, THEY WOULD. YOU'LL SEE.
THEY ALREADY LOVE YOUR BROTHER MORE THAN YOU.
IT'S TRUE. THEY'VE ALWAYS LOVED DANIEL BEST.
MY AUNTIE'S KEEPING AN EYE ON YOU.
SHE LOVES YOU EVEN THOUGH YOU DON'T KNOW IT YET, AND AIMS TO RESCUE YOU AND BRING YOU TO HER CABIN, WHERE ME AND YOU WILL LIVE LIKE SISTERS.
WILL I HAVE TO GO TO SCHOOL?
SCHOOL? NO, INDEED. OLD AUNTIE GOT NO USE FOR SCHOOL. SHE'LL TEACH YOU ALL YOU NEED TO KNOW.
I MUST GO.
The old woman sees the brother watching from the woods. He can't see her, but he knows someone is there.

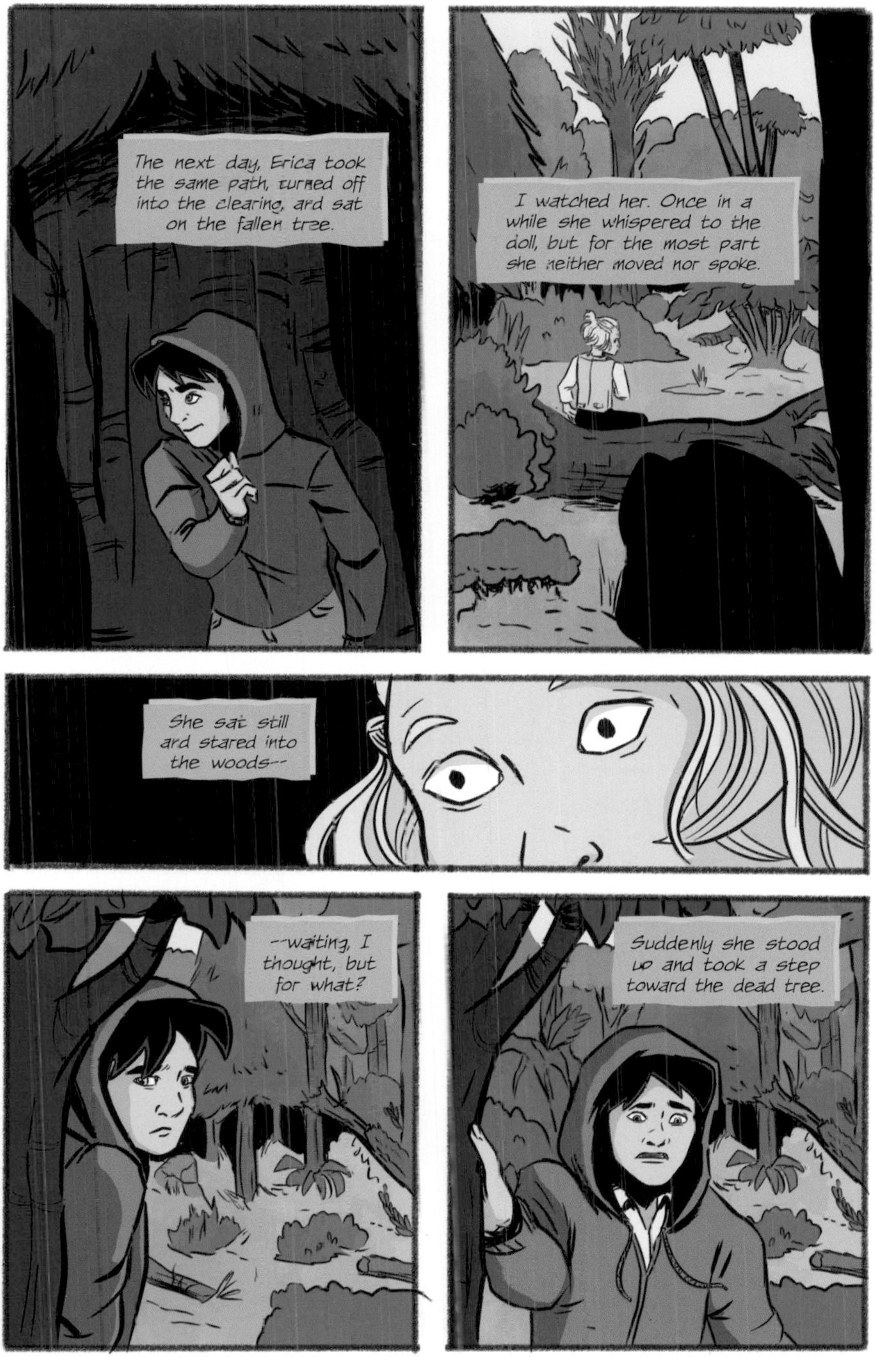
The next day, Erica took the same path, turned off into the clearing, and sat on the fallen tree.
I watched her. Once in a while she whispered to the doll, but for the most part she neither moved nor spoke.
She sat still and stared into the woods--
--waiting, I thought, but for what?
Suddenly she stood up and took a step toward the dead tree.

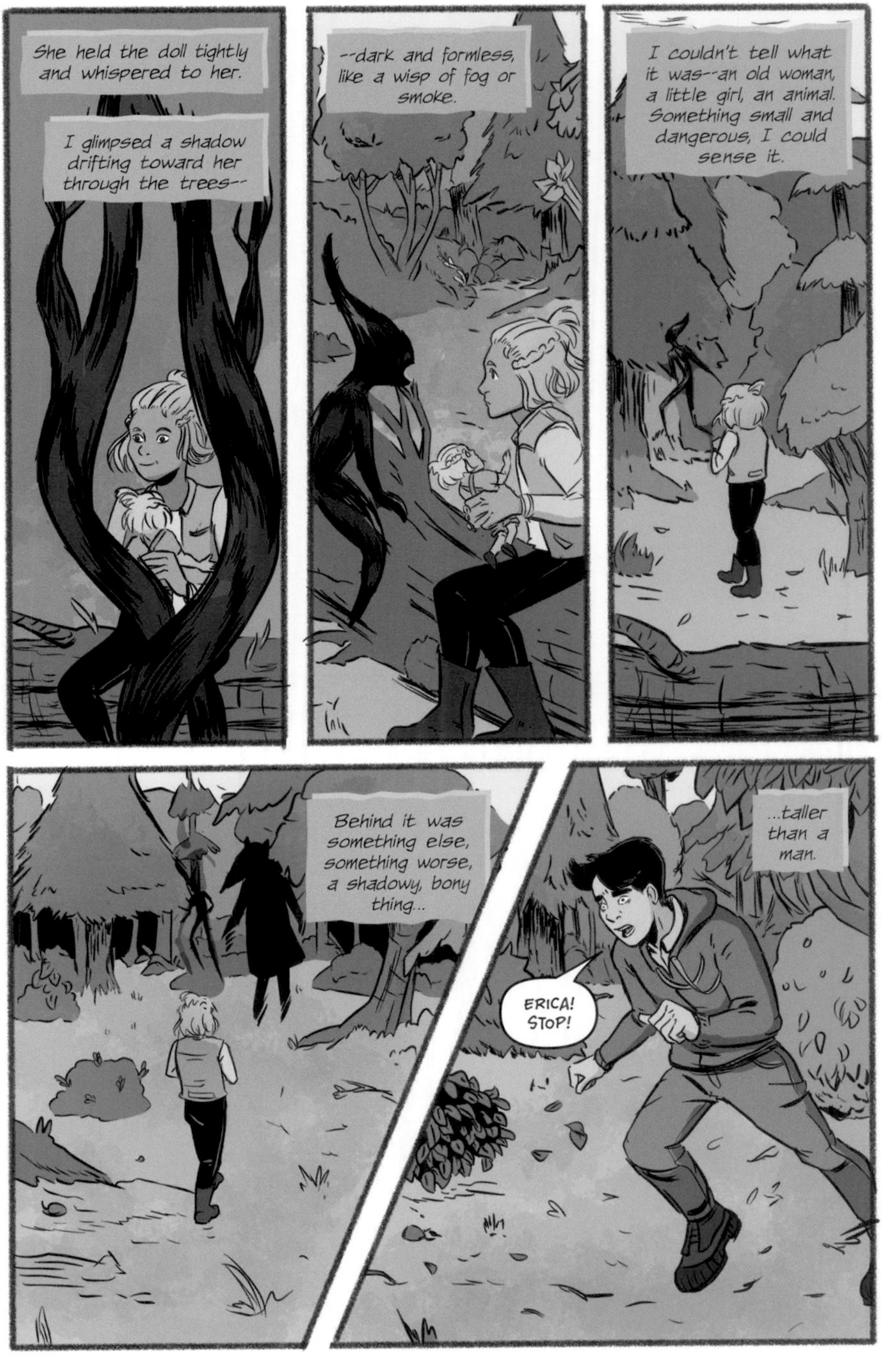
She held the doll tightly and whispered to her.
I glimpsed a shadow drifting toward her through the trees--
--dark and formless, like a wisp of fog or smoke.
I couldn't tell what it was--an old woman, a little girl, an animal. Something small and dangerous, I could sense it.
Behind it was something else, something worse, a shadowy, bony thing...
...taller than a man.
ERICA! STOP!

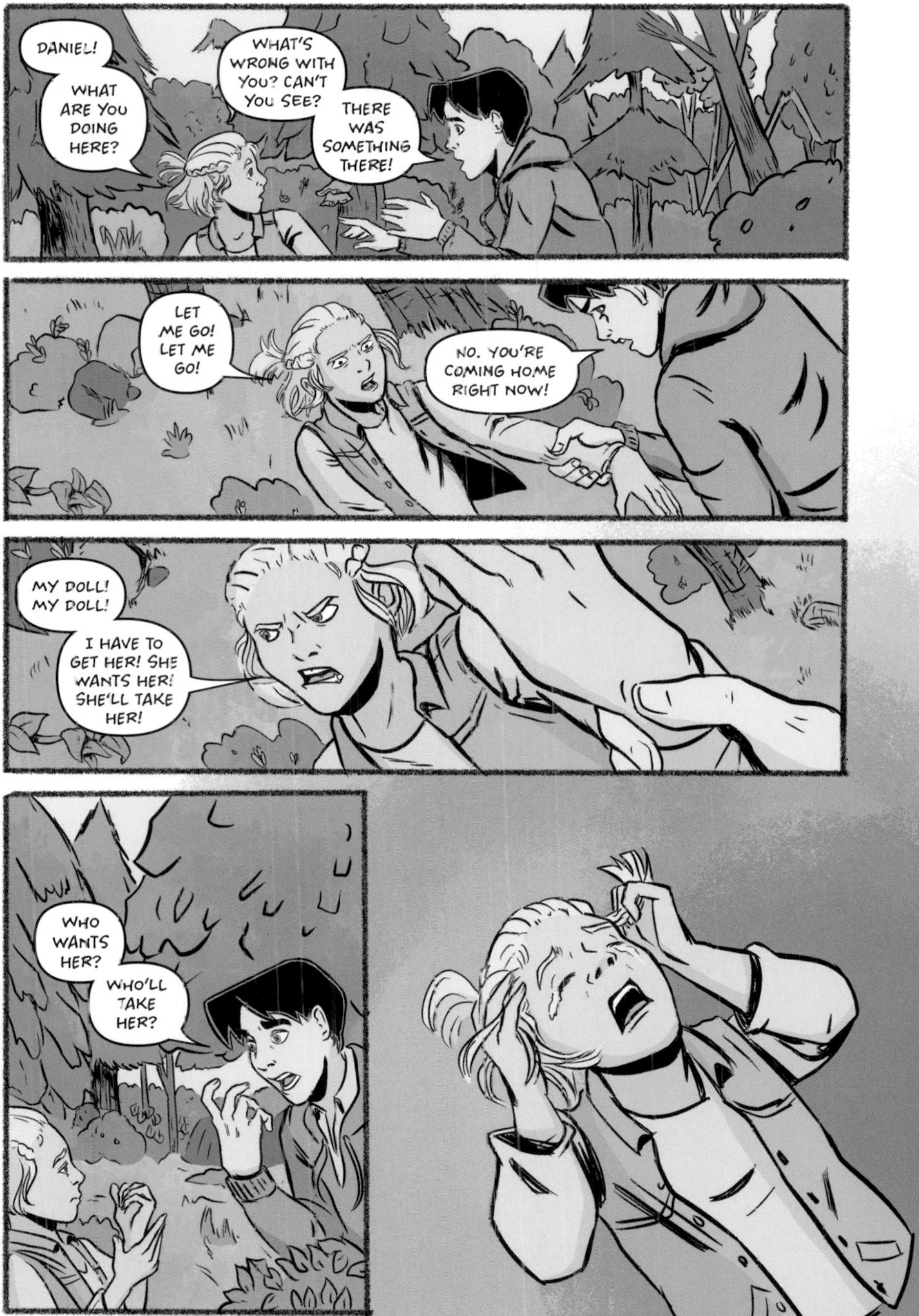
DANIEL!
WHAT ARE YOU DOING HERE?
WHAT'S WRONG WITH YOU? CAN'T YOU SEE?
THERE WAS SOMETHING THERE!
LET ME GO! LET ME GO!
NO. YOU'RE COMING HOME RIGHT NOW!
MY DOLL! MY DOLL!
I HAVE TO GET HER! SHE WANTS HER! SHE'LL TAKE HER!
WHO WANTS HER?
WHO'LL TAKE HER?

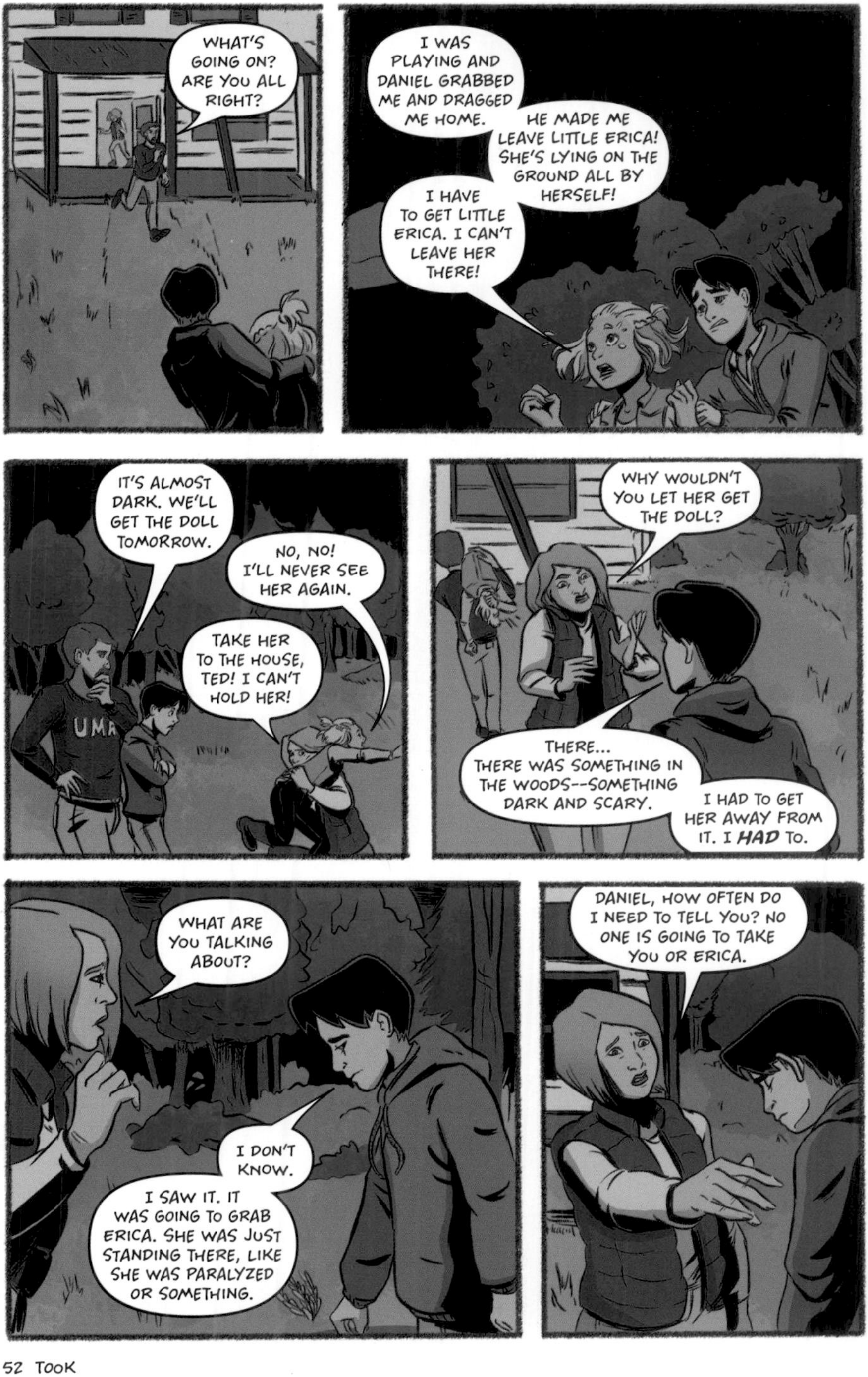
WHAT'S GOING ON? ARE YOU ALL RIGHT?
I WAS PLAYING AND DANIEL GRABBED ME AND DRAGGED ME HOME.
HE MADE ME LEAVE LITTLE ERICA! SHE'S LYING ON THE GROUND ALL BY HERSELF!
I HAVE TO GET LITTLE ERICA. I CAN'T LEAVE HER THERE!
IT'S ALMOST DARK. WE'LL GET THE DOLL TOMORROW.
NO, NO! I'LL NEVER SEE HER AGAIN.
TAKE HER TO THE HOUSE, TED! I CAN'T HOLD HER!
UMA
WHY WOULDN'T YOU LET HER GET THE DOLL?
THERE... THERE WAS SOMETHING IN THE WOODS--SOMETHING DARK AND SCARY.
I HAD TO GET HER AWAY FROM IT. I ***HAD*** TO.
WHAT ARE YOU TALKING ABOUT?
I DON'T KNOW.
I SAW IT. IT WAS GOING TO GRAB ERICA. SHE WAS JUST STANDING THERE, LIKE SHE WAS PARALYZED OR SOMETHING.
DANIEL, HOW OFTEN DO I NEED TO TELL YOU? NO ONE IS GOING TO TAKE YOU OR ERICA.

TOOK 53

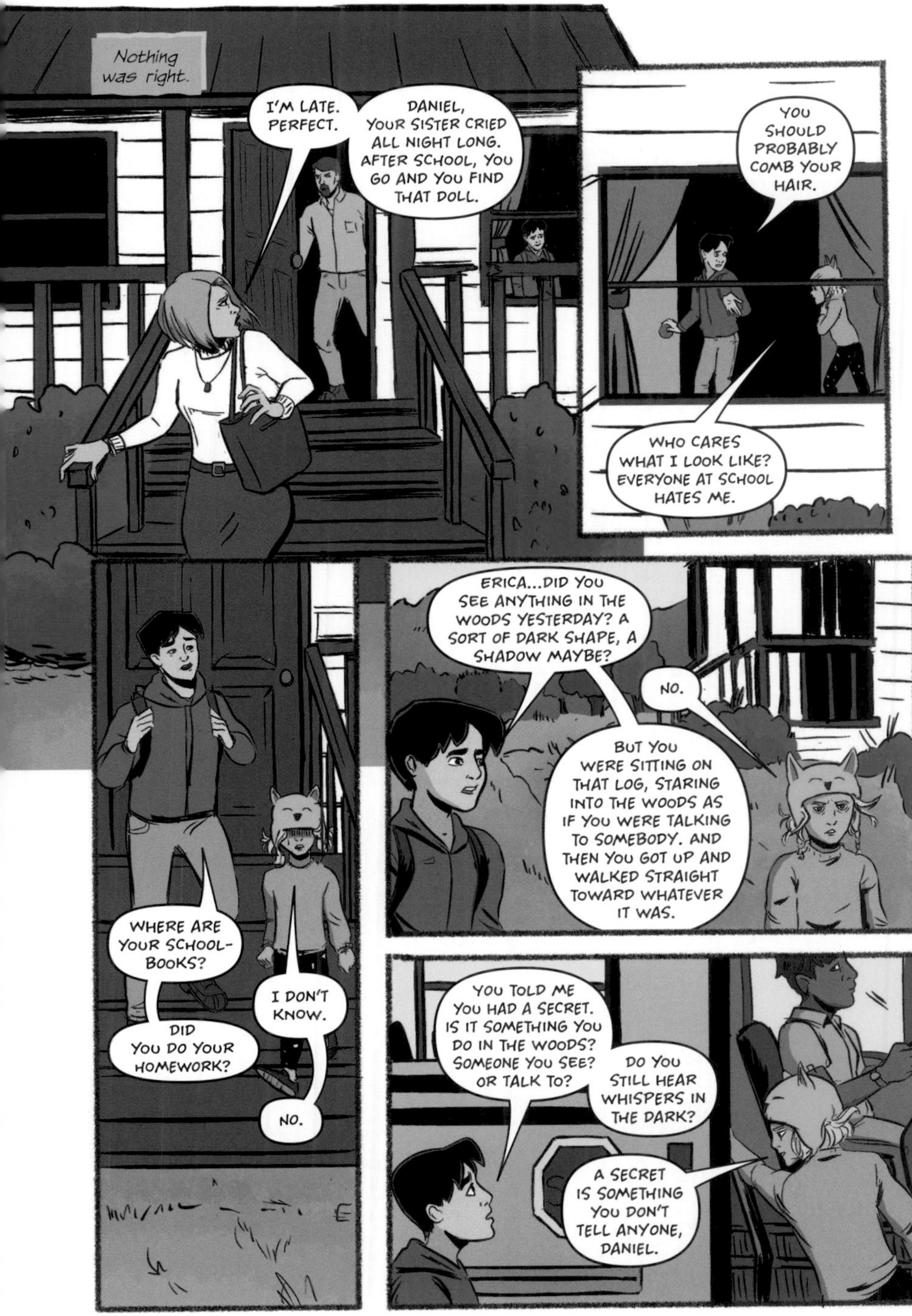
Nothing was right.
I'M LATE. PERFECT.
DANIEL, YOUR SISTER CRIED ALL NIGHT LONG. AFTER SCHOOL, YOU GO AND YOU FIND THAT DOLL.
YOU SHOULD PROBABLY COMB YOUR HAIR.
WHO CARES WHAT I LOOK LIKE? EVERYONE AT SCHOOL HATES ME.
WHERE ARE YOUR SCHOOL-BOOKS?
I DON'T KNOW.
DID YOU DO YOUR HOMEWORK?
NO.
ERICA...DID YOU SEE ANYTHING IN THE WOODS YESTERDAY? A SORT OF DARK SHAPE, A SHADOW MAYBE?
NO.
BUT YOU WERE SITTING ON THAT LOG, STARING INTO THE WOODS AS IF YOU WERE TALKING TO SOMEBODY. AND THEN YOU GOT UP AND WALKED STRAIGHT TOWARD WHATEVER IT WAS.
YOU TOLD ME YOU HAD A SECRET. IS IT SOMETHING YOU DO IN THE WOODS? SOMEONE YOU SEE? OR TALK TO?
DO YOU STILL HEAR WHISPERS IN THE DARK?
A SECRET IS SOMETHING YOU DON'T TELL ANYONE, DANIEL.

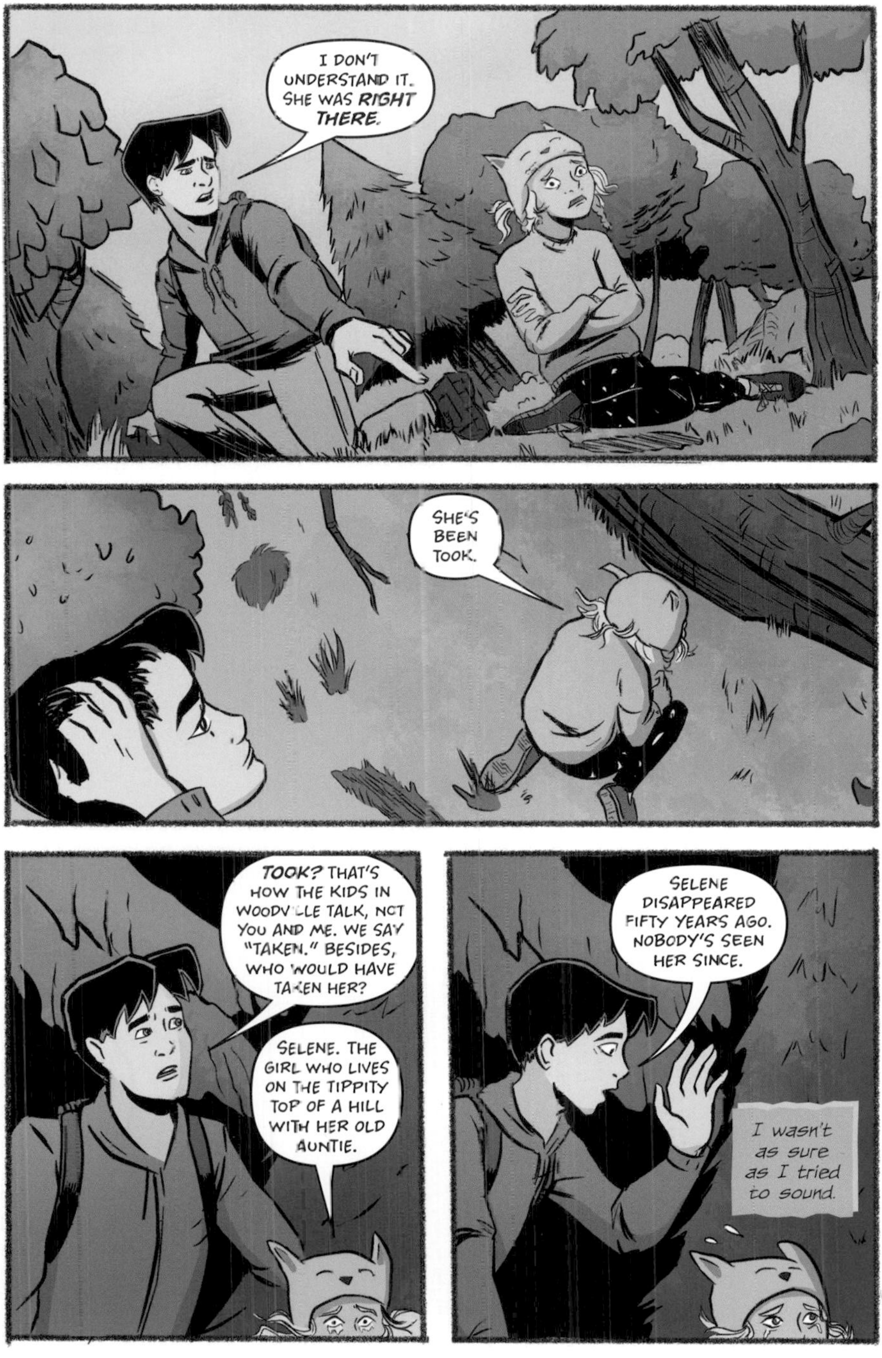
I DON'T UNDERSTAND IT. SHE WAS RIGHT THERE.
SHE'S BEEN TOOK.
TOOK? THAT'S HOW THE KIDS IN WOODVILLE TALK, NOT YOU AND ME. WE SAY "TAKEN." BESIDES, WHO WOULD HAVE TAKEN HER?
SELENE. THE GIRL WHO LIVES ON THE TIPPITY TOP OF A HILL WITH HER OLD AUNTIE.
SELENE DISAPPEARED FIFTY YEARS AGO. NOBODY'S SEEN HER SINCE.
I wasn't as sure as I tried to sound.

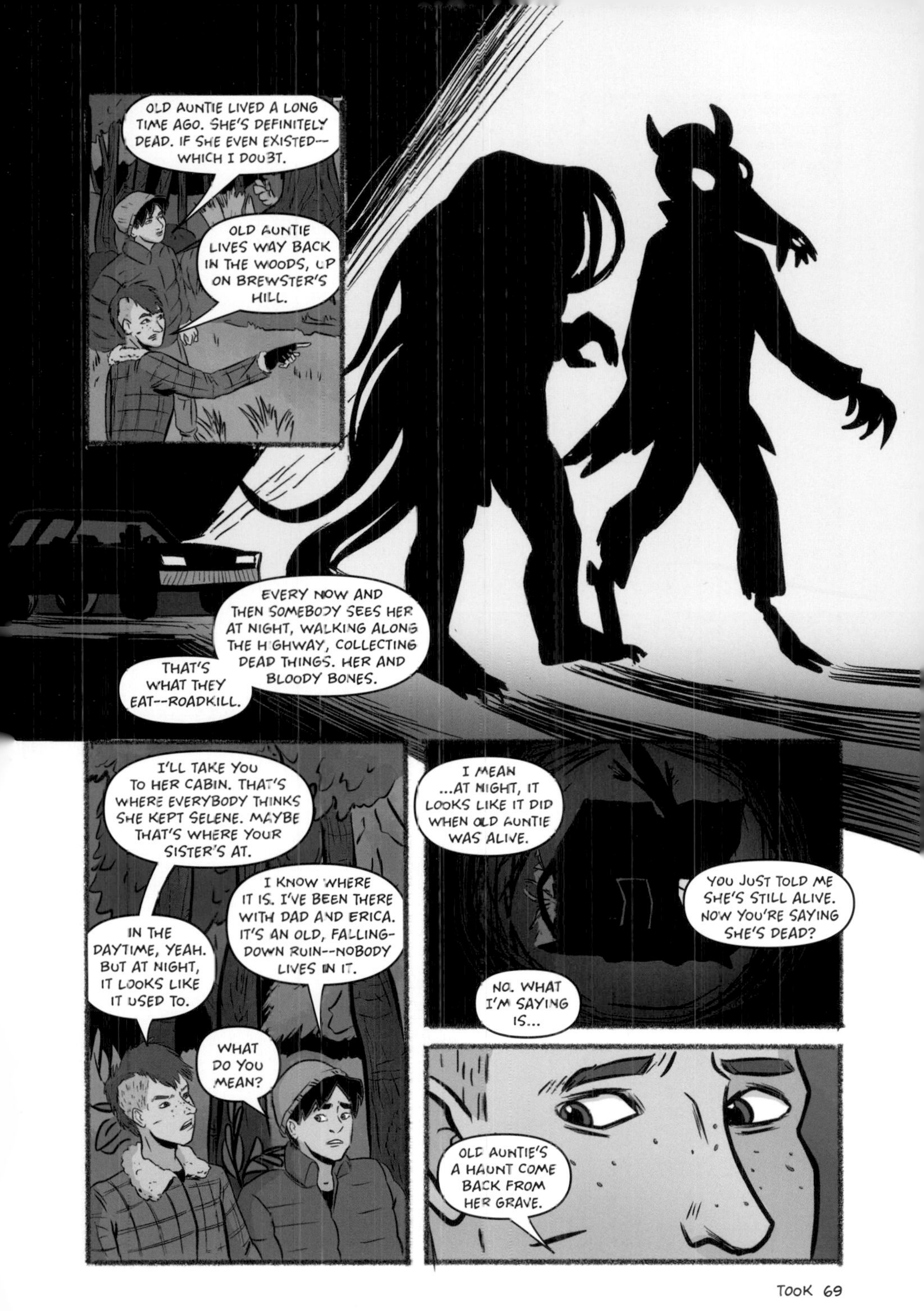

OLD AUNTIE LIVED A LONG TIME AGO. SHE'S DEFINITELY DEAD. IF SHE EVEN EXISTED--WHICH I DOUBT.
OLD AUNTIE LIVES WAY BACK IN THE WOODS, UP ON BREWSTER'S HILL.
EVERY NOW AND THEN SOMEBODY SEES HER AT NIGHT, WALKING ALONG THE HIGHWAY, COLLECTING DEAD THINGS. HER AND BLOODY BONES.
THAT'S WHAT THEY EAT--ROADKILL.
I'LL TAKE YOU TO HER CABIN. THAT'S WHERE EVERYBODY THINKS SHE KEPT SELENE. MAYBE THAT'S WHERE YOUR SISTER'S AT.
I KNOW WHERE IT IS. I'VE BEEN THERE WITH DAD AND ERICA. IT'S AN OLD, FALLING-DOWN RUIN--NOBODY LIVES IN IT.
IN THE DAYTIME, YEAH. BUT AT NIGHT, IT LOOKS LIKE IT USED TO.
WHAT DO YOU MEAN?
I MEAN ...AT NIGHT, IT LOOKS LIKE IT DID WHEN OLD AUNTIE WAS ALIVE.
YOU JUST TOLD ME SHE'S STILL ALIVE. NOW YOU'RE SAYING SHE'S DEAD?
NO. WHAT I'M SAYING IS...
OLD AUNTIE'S A HAUNT COME BACK FROM HER GRAVE.

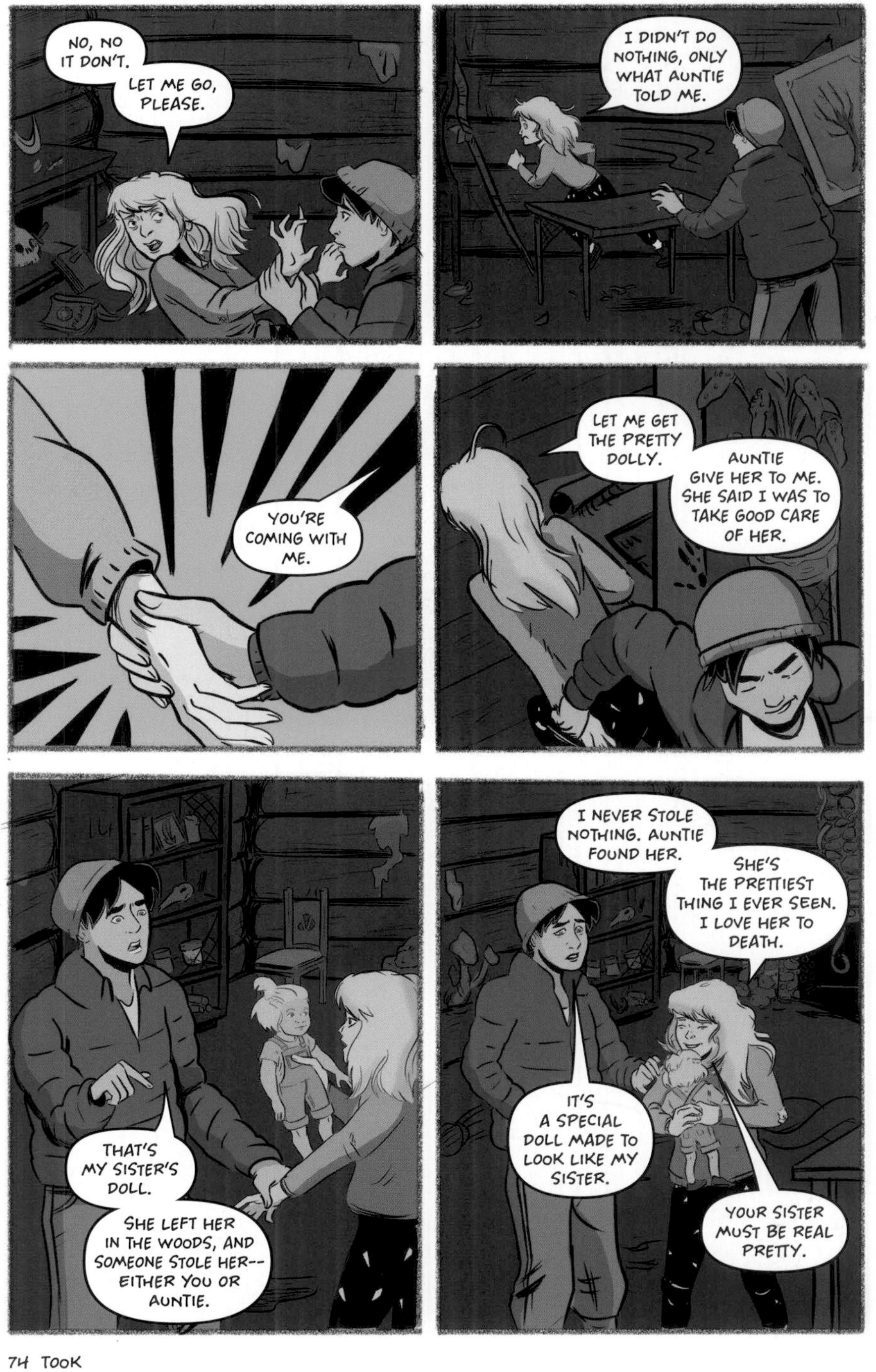
NO, NO IT DON'T.
LET ME GO, PLEASE.
I DIDN'T DO NOTHING, ONLY WHAT AUNTIE TOLD ME.
YOU'RE COMING WITH ME.
LET ME GET THE PRETTY DOLLY.
AUNTIE GIVE HER TO ME. SHE SAID I WAS TO TAKE GOOD CARE OF HER.
THAT'S MY SISTER'S DOLL.
SHE LEFT HER IN THE WOODS, AND SOMEONE STOLE HER-- EITHER YOU OR AUNTIE.
I NEVER STOLE NOTHING. AUNTIE FOUND HER.
SHE'S THE PRETTIEST THING I EVER SEEN. I LOVE HER TO DEATH.
IT'S A SPECIAL DOLL MADE TO LOOK LIKE MY SISTER.
YOUR SISTER MUST BE REAL PRETTY.

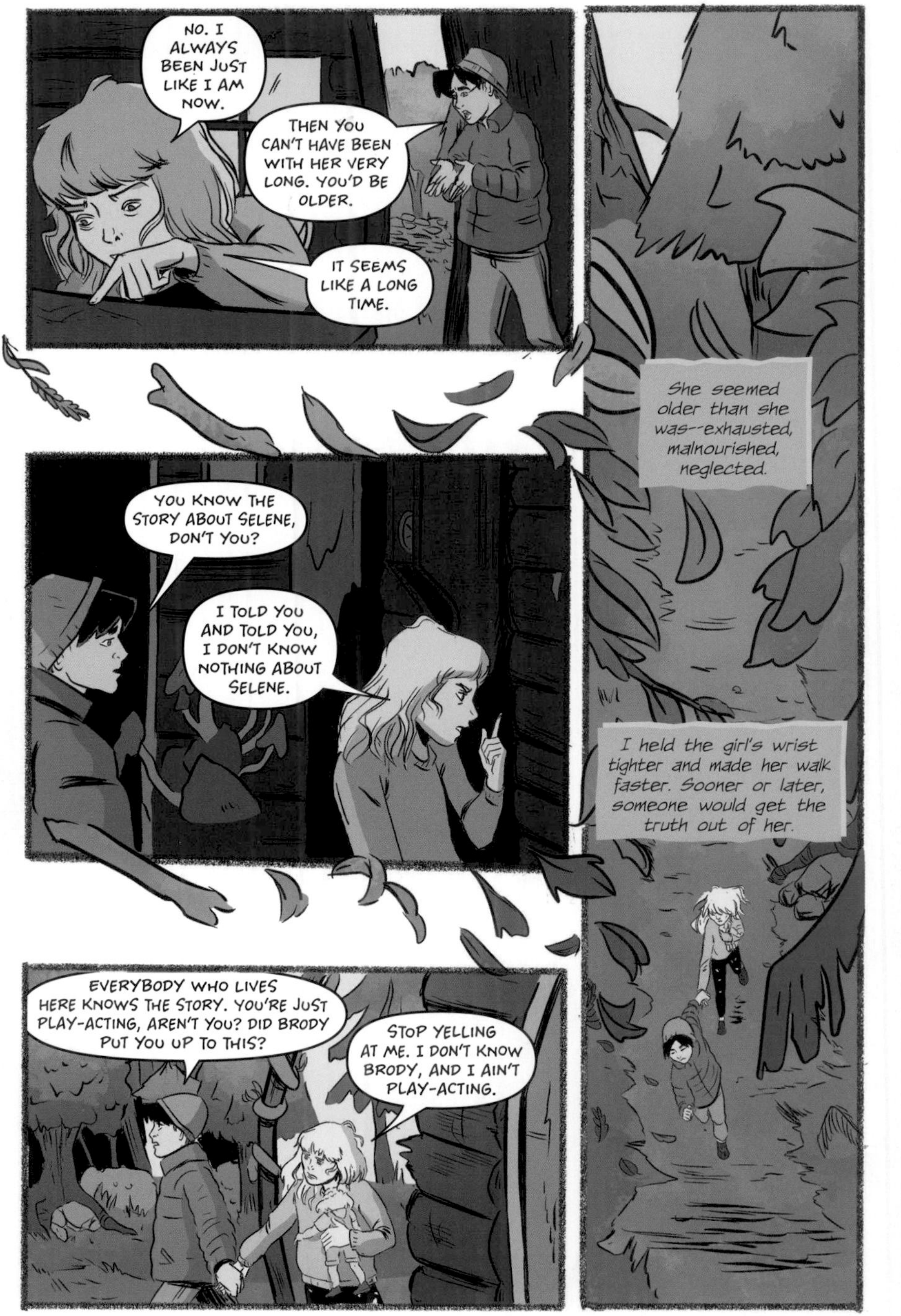

NO. I ALWAYS BEEN JUST LIKE I AM NOW.
THEN YOU CAN'T HAVE BEEN WITH HER VERY LONG. YOU'D BE OLDER.
IT SEEMS LIKE A LONG TIME.
She seemed older than she was--exhausted, malnourished, neglected.
YOU KNOW THE STORY ABOUT SELENE, DON'T YOU?
I TOLD YOU AND TOLD YOU, I DON'T KNOW NOTHING ABOUT SELENE.
I held the girl's wrist tighter and made her walk faster. Sooner or later, someone would get the truth out of her.
EVERYBODY WHO LIVES HERE KNOWS THE STORY. YOU'RE JUST PLAY-ACTING, AREN'T YOU? DID BRODY PUT YOU UP TO THIS?
STOP YELLING AT ME. I DON'T KNOW BRODY, AND I AIN'T PLAY-ACTING.

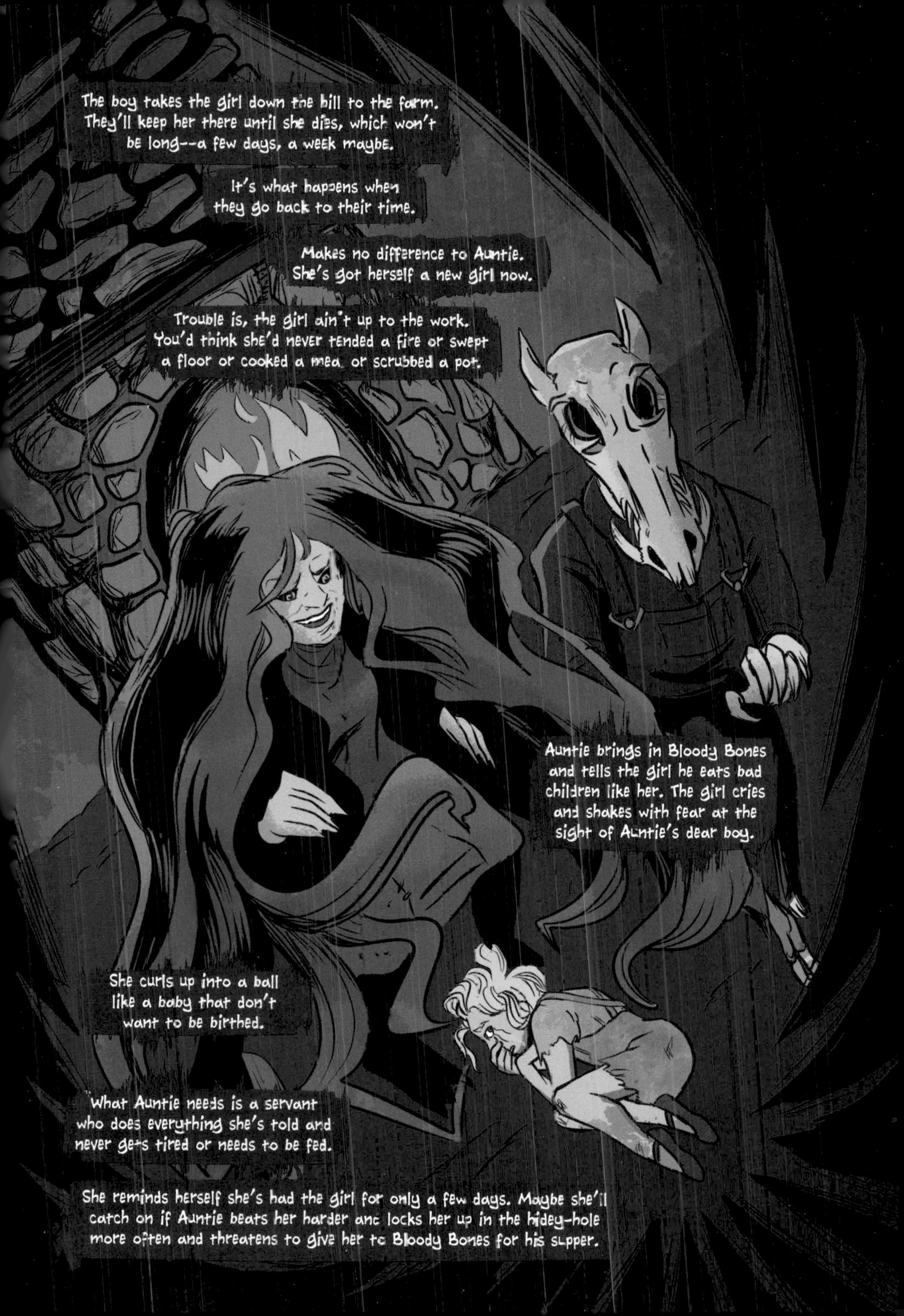
The boy takes the girl down the hill to the farm. They'll keep her there until she dies, which won't be long--a few days, a week maybe.
It's what happens when they go back to their time.
Makes no difference to Auntie. She's got herself a new girl now.
Trouble is, the girl ain't up to the work. You'd think she'd never tended a fire or swept a floor or cooked a meal or scrubbed a pot.
Auntie brings in Bloody Bones and tells the girl he eats bad children like her. The girl cries and shakes with fear at the sight of Auntie's dear boy.
She curls up into a ball like a baby that don't want to be birthed.
What Auntie needs is a servant who does everything she's told and never gets tired or needs to be fed.
She reminds herself she's had the girl for only a few days. Maybe she'll catch on if Auntie beats her harder and locks her up in the hidey-hole more often and threatens to give her to Bloody Bones for his supper.

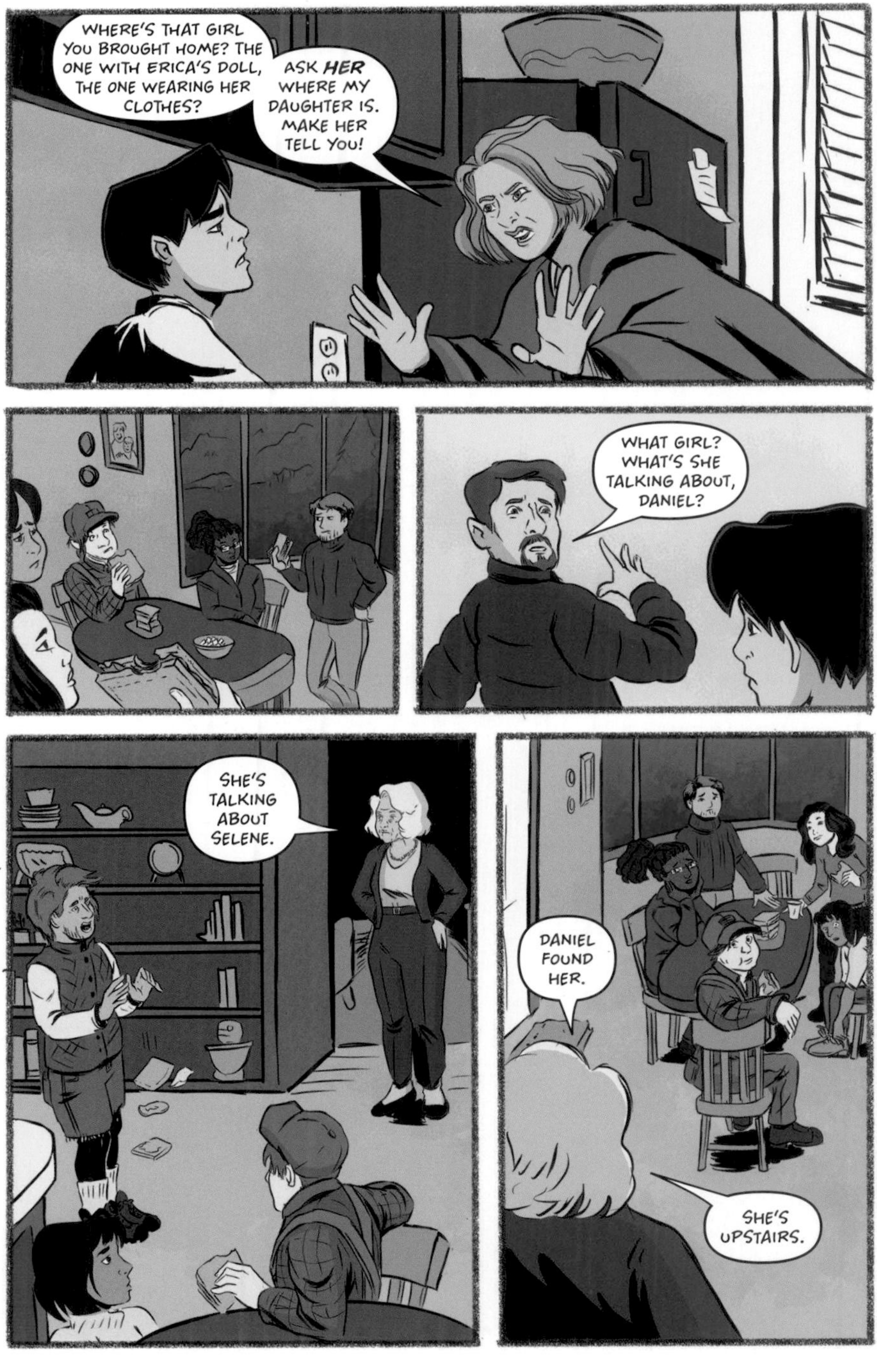
WHERE'S THAT GIRL YOU BROUGHT HOME? THE ONE WITH ERICA'S DOLL, THE ONE WEARING HER CLOTHES?
ASK **HER** WHERE MY DAUGHTER IS. MAKE HER TELL YOU!
WHAT GIRL? WHAT'S SHE TALKING ABOUT, DANIEL?
SHE'S TALKING ABOUT SELENE.
DANIEL FOUND HER.
SHE'S UPSTAIRS.

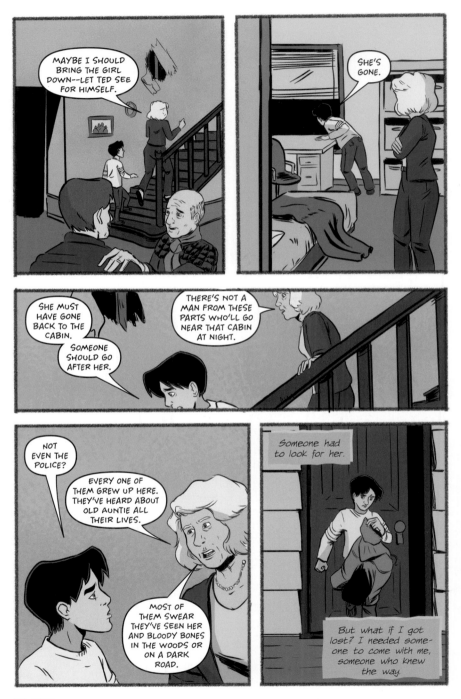

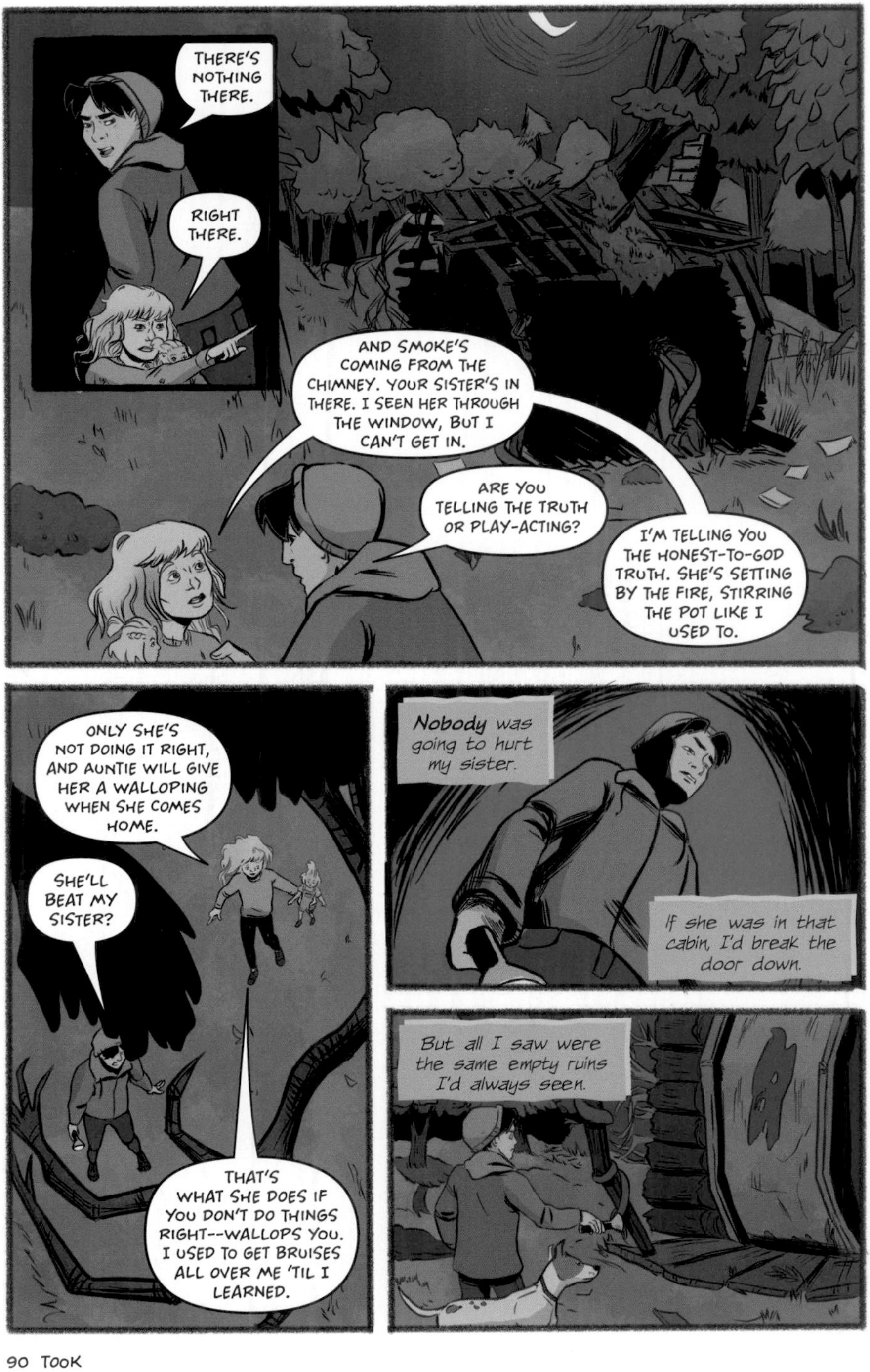
THERE'S NOTHING THERE.
RIGHT THERE.
AND SMOKE'S COMING FROM THE CHIMNEY. YOUR SISTER'S IN THERE. I SEEN HER THROUGH THE WINDOW, BUT I CAN'T GET IN.
ARE YOU TELLING THE TRUTH OR PLAY-ACTING?
I'M TELLING YOU THE HONEST-TO-GOD TRUTH. SHE'S SETTING BY THE FIRE, STIRRING THE POT LIKE I USED TO.
ONLY SHE'S NOT DOING IT RIGHT, AND AUNTIE WILL GIVE HER A WALLOPING WHEN SHE COMES HOME.
SHE'LL BEAT MY SISTER?
THAT'S WHAT SHE DOES IF YOU DON'T DO THINGS RIGHT--WALLOPS YOU. I USED TO GET BRUISES ALL OVER ME 'TIL I LEARNED.
Nobody was going to hurt my sister.
If she was in that cabin, I'd break the door down.
But all I saw were the same empty ruins I'd always seen.

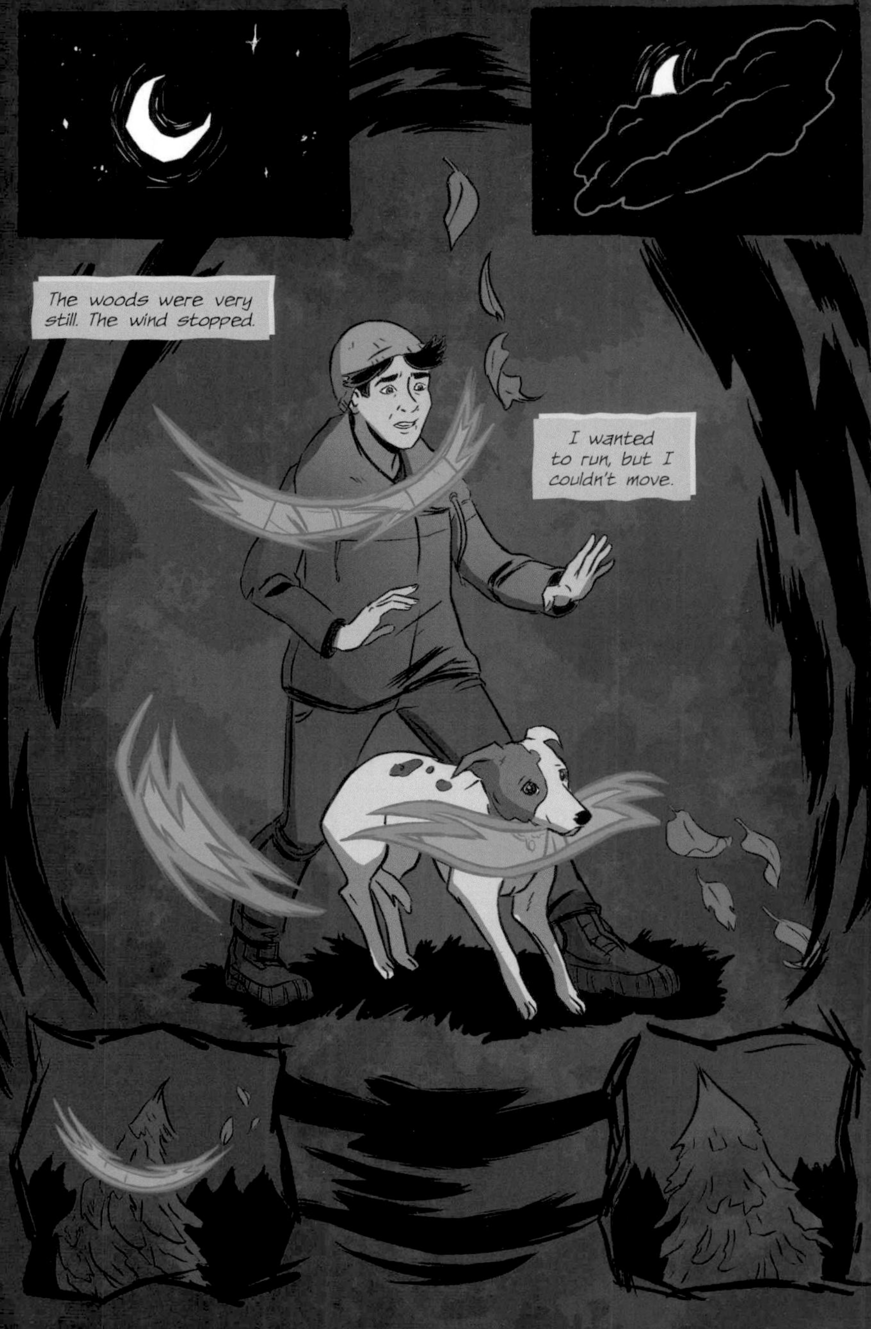
The woods were very still. The wind stopped.
I wanted to run, but I couldn't move.

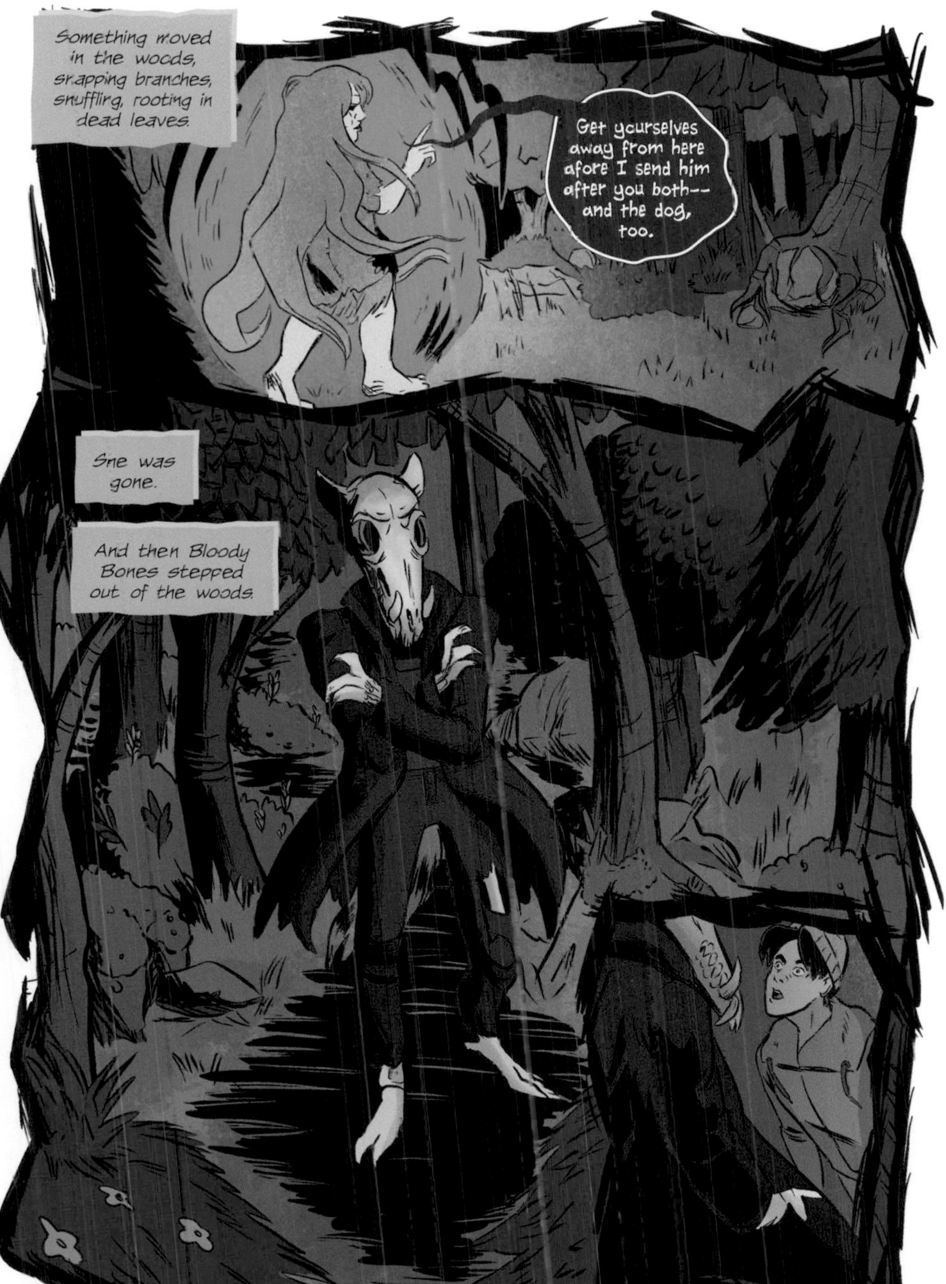
Something moved in the woods, snapping branches, snuffling, rooting in dead leaves.
Get yourselves away from here afore I send him after you both--and the dog, too.
She was gone.
And then Bloody Bones stepped out of the woods.

Her eyes go to the window.

Your brother won't be back--my dear boy has scairt him off.

But if'n he does come back, you won't go with him 'cause you love your old auntie and you know she loves you. Say you love me.

I LOVE YOU SO MUCH, AUNTIE.

Auntie's dear boy peers in. But he's not her brother. Or is he? She doesn't know. She doesn't know anything.

The cabin reeks of deadly nightshade, henbane, hemlock, and foxglove--poisons.

In dark corners, bats nest and black widows lurk. The girl is afraid to sweep away their webs.

But most of all she's afraid of Bloody Bones. She hates Auntie's dear boy.

But she doesn't hate Auntie. Oh, no. She loves Auntie.

Auntie is all she has to keep her safe from Bloody Bones.

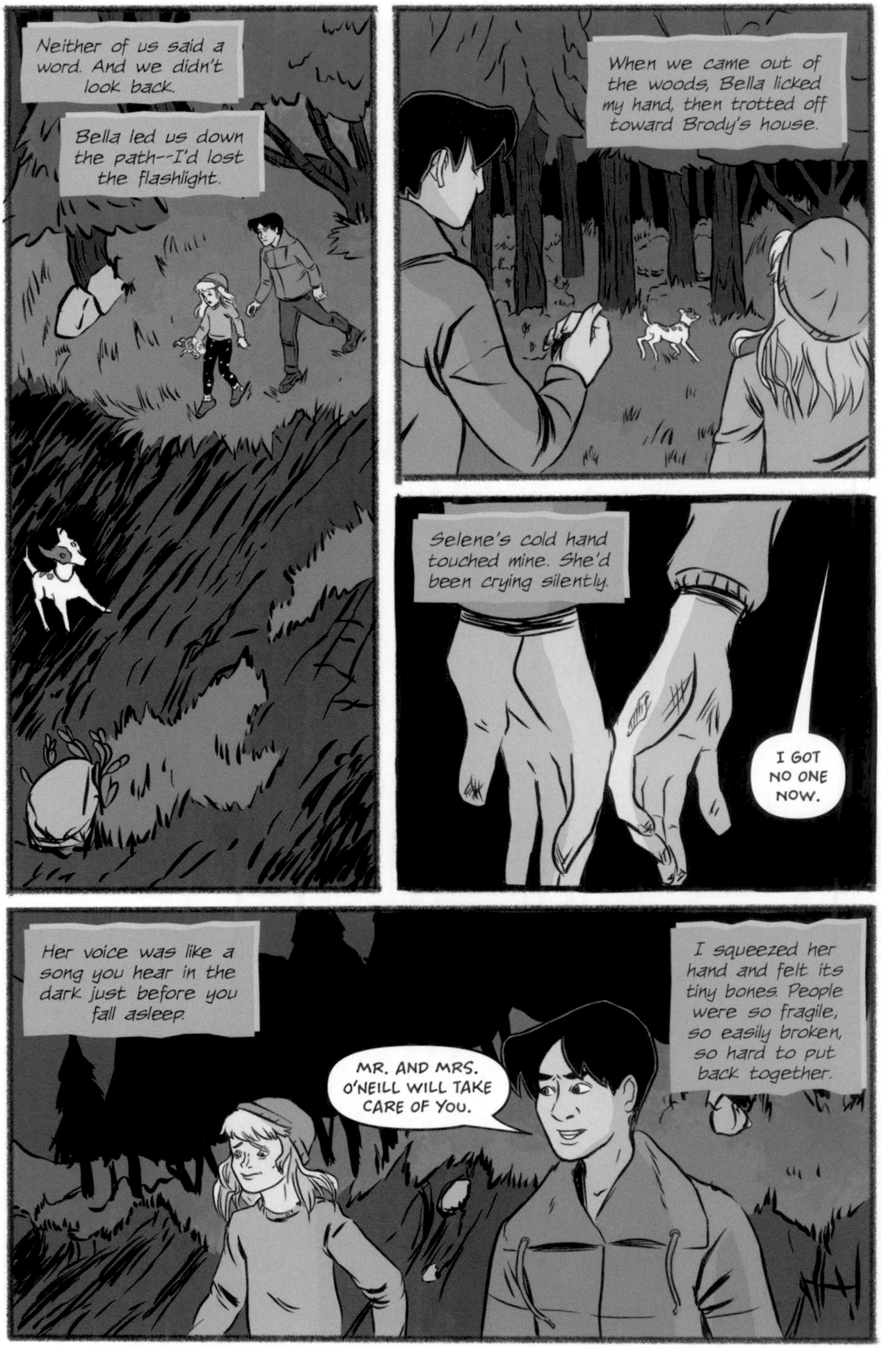
Neither of us said a word. And we didn't look back.
Bella led us down the path--I'd lost the flashlight.
When we came out of the woods, Bella licked my hand, then trotted off toward Brody's house.
Selene's cold hand touched mine. She'd been crying silently.
I GOT NO ONE NOW.
Her voice was like a song you hear in the dark just before you fall asleep.
I squeezed her hand and felt its tiny bones. People were so fragile, so easily broken, so hard to put back together.
MR. AND MRS. O'NEILL WILL TAKE CARE OF YOU.

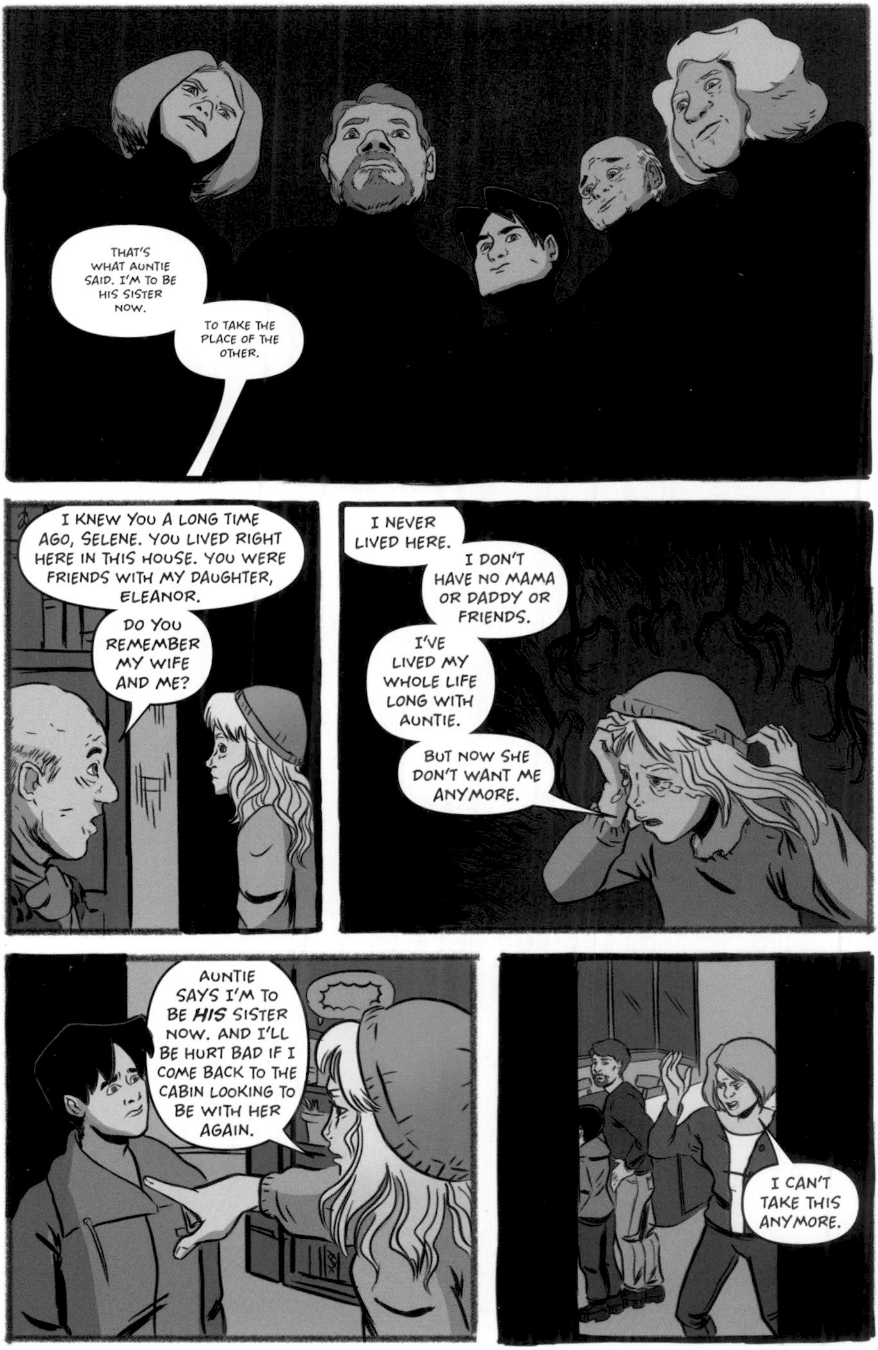
THAT'S WHAT AUNTIE SAID. I'M TO BE HIS SISTER NOW.
TO TAKE THE PLACE OF THE OTHER.
I KNEW YOU A LONG TIME AGO, SELENE. YOU LIVED RIGHT HERE IN THIS HOUSE. YOU WERE FRIENDS WITH MY DAUGHTER, ELEANOR.
DO YOU REMEMBER MY WIFE AND ME?
I NEVER LIVED HERE.
I DON'T HAVE NO MAMA OR DADDY OR FRIENDS.
I'VE LIVED MY WHOLE LIFE LONG WITH AUNTIE.
BUT NOW SHE DON'T WANT ME ANYMORE.
AUNTIE SAYS I'M TO BE ***HIS*** SISTER NOW. AND I'LL BE HURT BAD IF I COME BACK TO THE CABIN LOOKING TO BE WITH HER AGAIN.
I CAN'T TAKE THIS ANYMORE.

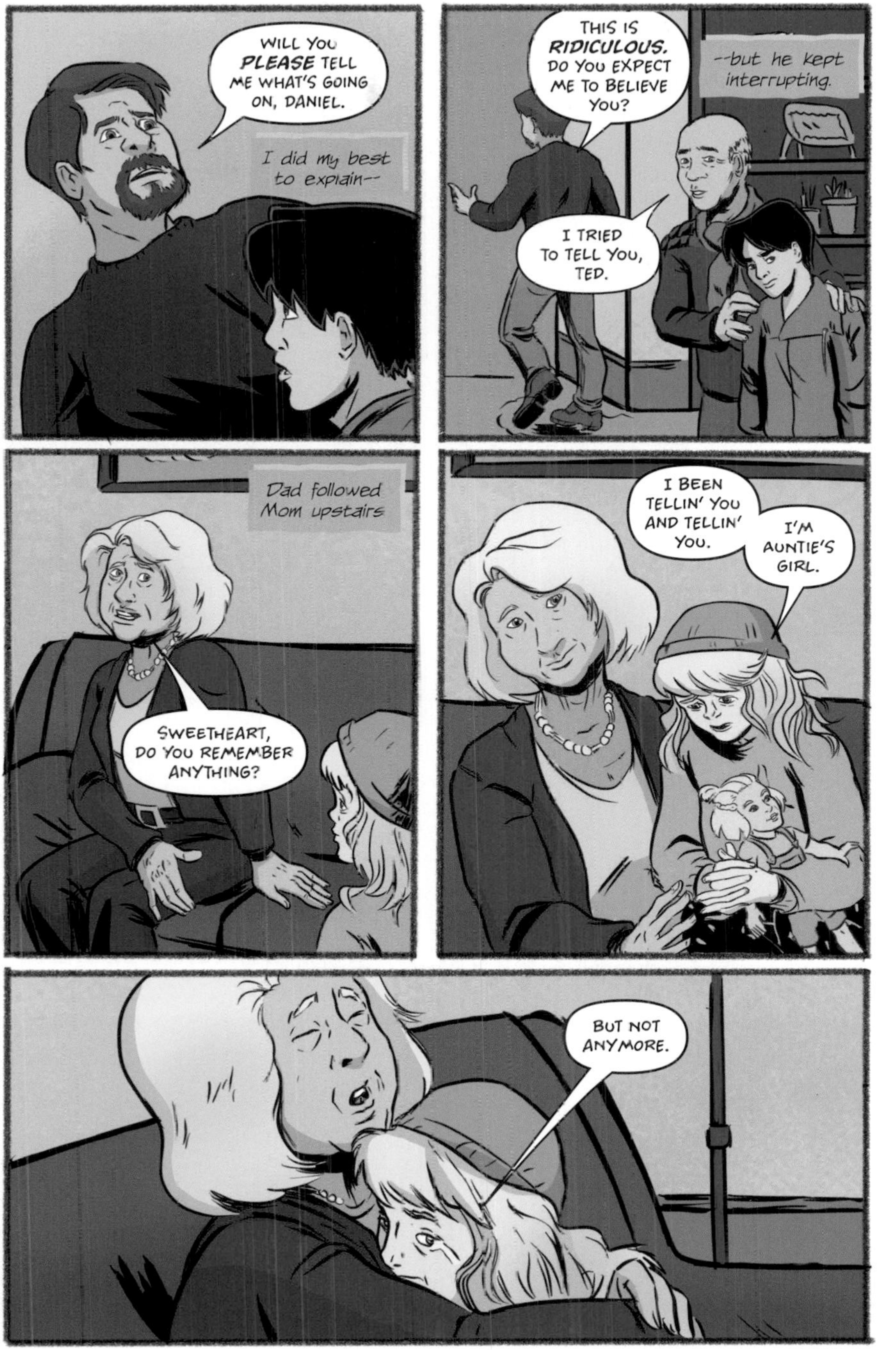
WILL YOU PLEASE TELL ME WHAT'S GOING ON, DANIEL.
I did my best to expiain--
THIS IS RIDICULOUS. DO YOU EXPECT ME TO BELIEVE YOU?
--but he kept interrupting.
I TRIED TO TELL YOU, TED.
Dad followed Mom upstairs
SWEETHEART, DO YOU REMEMBER ANYTHING?
I BEEN TELLIN' YOU AND TELLIN' YOU.
I'M AUNTIE'S GIRL.
BUT NOT ANYMORE.

I stared off into the woods and tried not to think about what I'd seen.
HE...HE JUST STOOD THERE AND LOOKED AT US.
AND THEN OLD AUNTIE WHISTLED FOR HIM.
HE'S...
HE'S... HORRIBLE, JUST LIKE YOU SAID.
YOU MUST BE REALLY BRAVE OR REALLY STUPID. BUT I'M GLAD YOU BRUNG MY DOG HOME SAFE.
We stood staring at the trees, as if we expected to see Bloody Bones or Old Auntie.
IS SELENE AT YOUR HOUSE?
THE O'NEILLS TOOK HER HOME WITH THEM. THAT'S WHERE I'M GOING.
CAN I COME? I WANT TO SEE HER.
Snow began falling. Brody caught snowflakes on his tongue like a kid.
Even though I was half-crazy with worry about my sister, I did the same.

BRODY, WHAT DO YOU KNOW ABOUT THE OLD WOMAN WHO LIVES DOWN AT THE END OF RAILROAD AVENUE?

MISS PERKINS? SHE'S **CRAZY**, THAT'S WHAT.

"Nobody has nothing to do with her unless it's something secret like, like—well, I don't exactly know what.

"But every **cat** and **dog** that goes missing ends up in her stew pot.

"And maybe other things, too."

I remembered the name Perkins from the bus. They'd called her a "conjure woman."

I'VE HEARD PLENTY OF THOSE STORIES. BUT I'VE ALSO HEARD SHE'S A DESCENDANT OF OLD AUNTIE AND KNOWS A THING OR TWO ABOUT CONJURING HERSELF.

Just then, the door opened and a woman came in.

It was Eleanor, the O'Neills' daughter.

She turned so pale as she stared at Selene, I thought she might faint.

Selene didn't so much as glance at her.

MY GOD, MOTHER.

SHE'S FIFTY-SEVEN YEARS OLD, BUT SHE LOOKS LIKE SHE DID ON THE DAY SHE DISAPPEARED.

I KNOW YOU WARNED ME BUT...**HOW CAN THAT BE?**

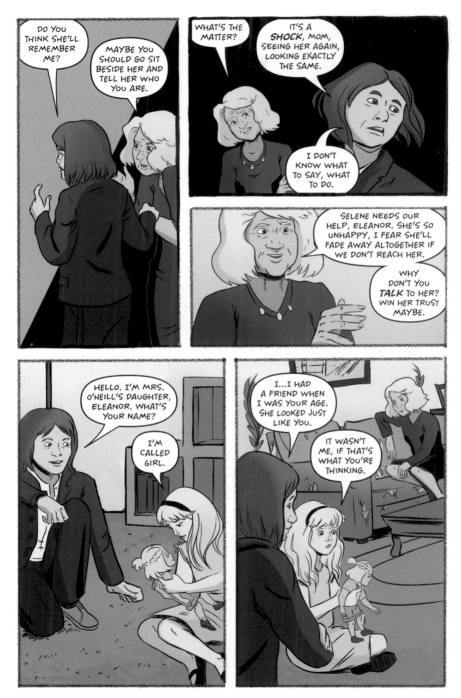

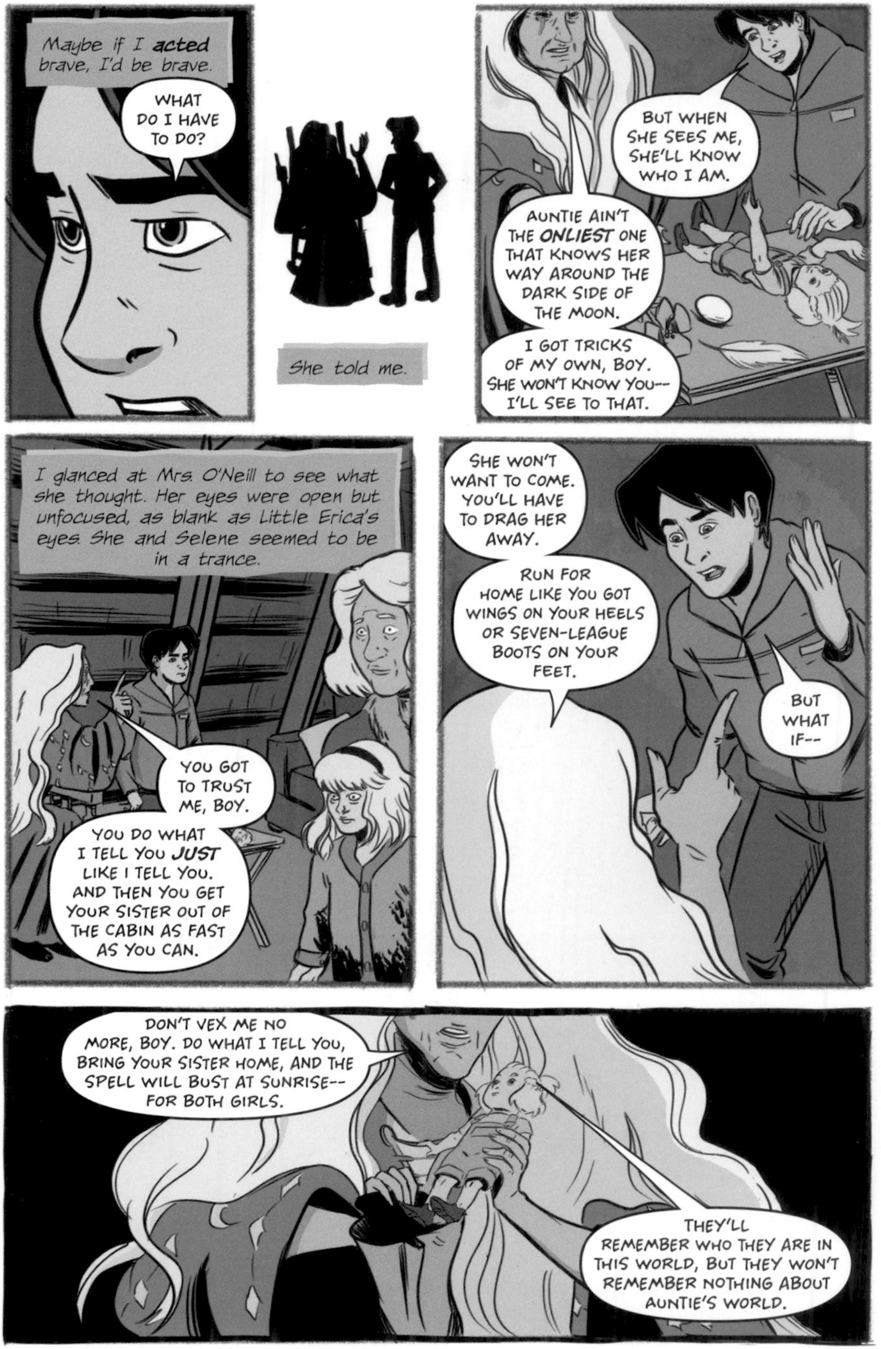
Maybe if I **acted** brave, I'd be brave.
WHAT DO I HAVE TO DO?
She told me.
BUT WHEN SHE SEES ME, SHE'LL KNOW WHO I AM.
AUNTIE AIN'T THE ***ONLIEST*** ONE THAT KNOWS HER WAY AROUND THE DARK SIDE OF THE MOON.
I GOT TRICKS OF MY OWN, BOY. SHE WON'T KNOW YOU-- I'LL SEE TO THAT.
I glanced at Mrs. O'Neill to see what she thought. Her eyes were open but unfocused, as blank as Little Erica's eyes. She and Selene seemed to be in a trance.
YOU GOT TO TRUST ME, BOY.
YOU DO WHAT I TELL YOU ***JUST*** LIKE I TELL YOU. AND THEN YOU GET YOUR SISTER OUT OF THE CABIN AS FAST AS YOU CAN.
SHE WON'T WANT TO COME. YOU'LL HAVE TO DRAG HER AWAY.
RUN FOR HOME LIKE YOU GOT WINGS ON YOUR HEELS OR SEVEN-LEAGUE BOOTS ON YOUR FEET.
BUT WHAT IF--
DON'T VEX ME NO MORE, BOY. DO WHAT I TELL YOU, BRING YOUR SISTER HOME, AND THE SPELL WILL BUST AT SUNRISE-- FOR BOTH GIRLS.
THEY'LL REMEMBER WHO THEY ARE IN THIS WORLD, BUT THEY WON'T REMEMBER NOTHING ABOUT AUNTIE'S WORLD.

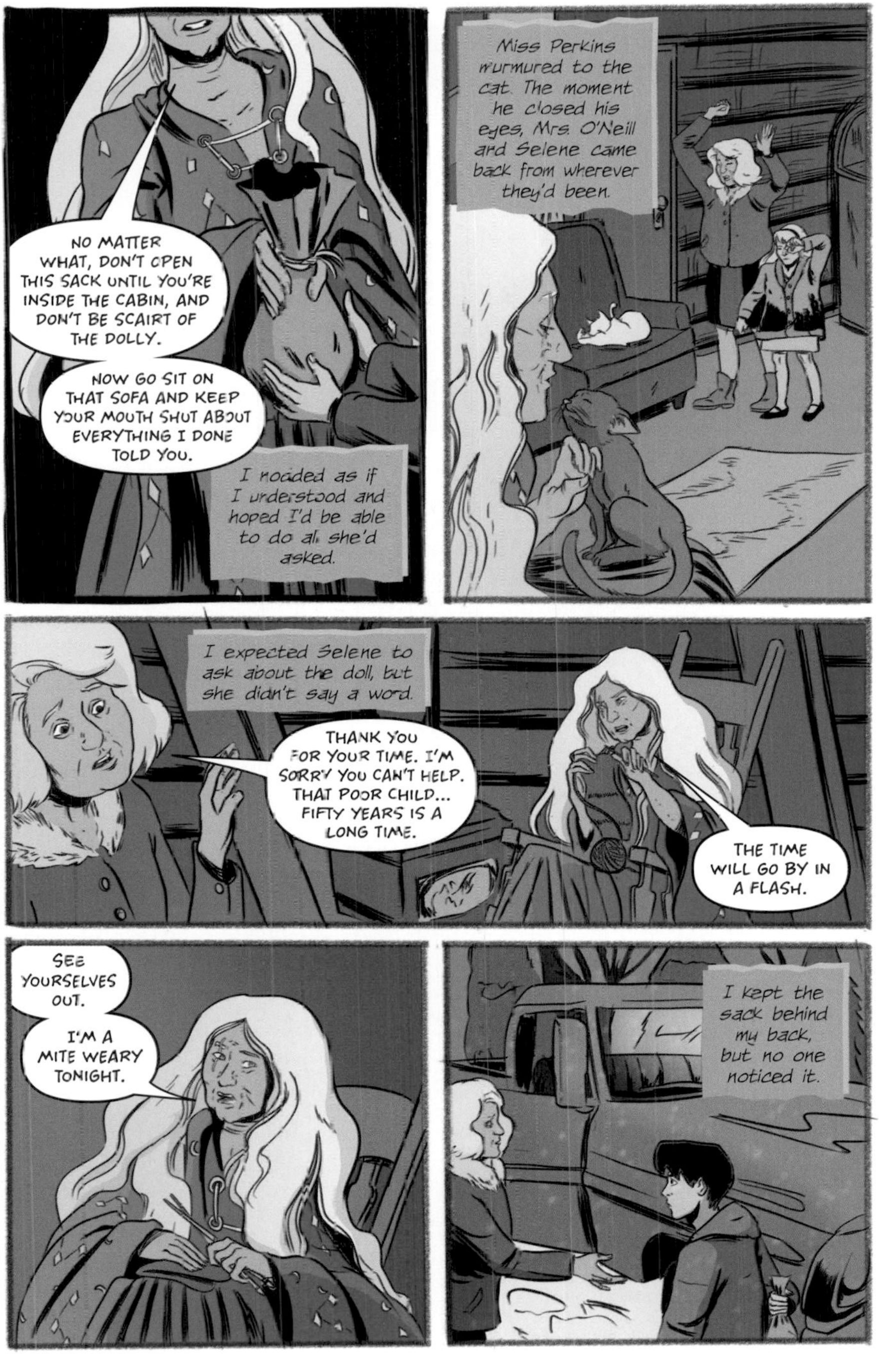
NO MATTER WHAT, DON'T OPEN THIS SACK UNTIL YOU'RE INSIDE THE CABIN, AND DON'T BE SCAIRT OF THE DOLLY.
NOW GO SIT ON THAT SOFA AND KEEP YOUR MOUTH SHUT ABOUT EVERYTHING I DONE TOLD YOU.
I nodded as if I understood and hoped I'd be able to do all she'd asked.
Miss Perkins murmured to the cat. The moment he closed his eyes, Mrs. O'Neill and Selene came back from wherever they'd been.
I expected Selene to ask about the doll, but she didn't say a word.
THANK YOU FOR YOUR TIME. I'M SORRY YOU CAN'T HELP. THAT POOR CHILD... FIFTY YEARS IS A LONG TIME.
THE TIME WILL GO BY IN A FLASH.
SEE YOURSELVES OUT.
I'M A MITE WEARY TONIGHT.
I kept the sack behind my back, but no one noticed it.

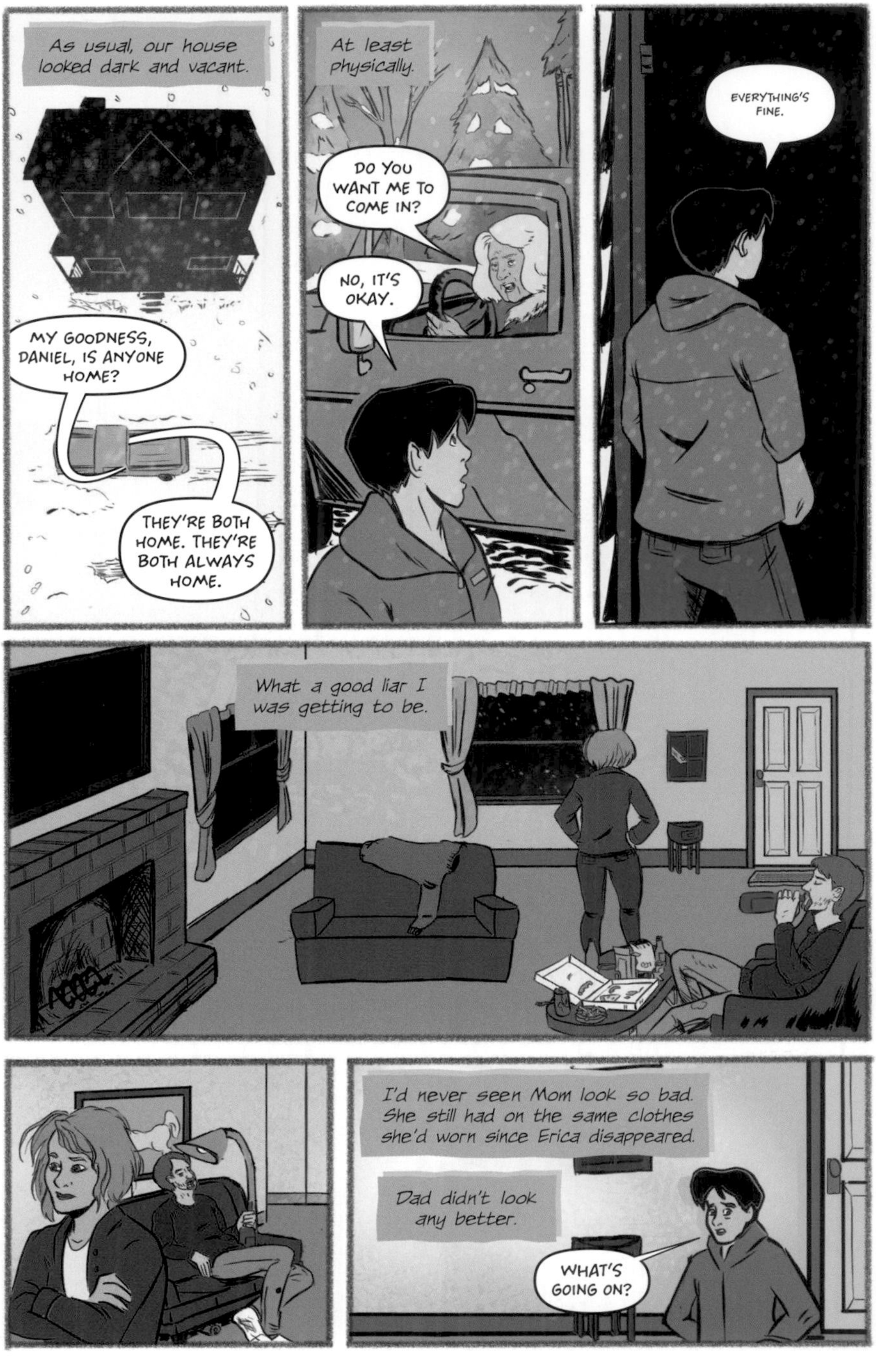
As usual, our house looked dark and vacant.
MY GOODNESS, DANIEL, IS ANYONE HOME?
THEY'RE BOTH HOME. THEY'RE BOTH ALWAYS HOME.
At least physically.
DO YOU WANT ME TO COME IN?
NO, IT'S OKAY.
EVERYTHING'S FINE.
What a good liar I was getting to be.
I'd never seen Mom look so bad. She still had on the same clothes she'd worn since Erica disappeared.
Dad didn't look any better.
WHAT'S GOING ON?

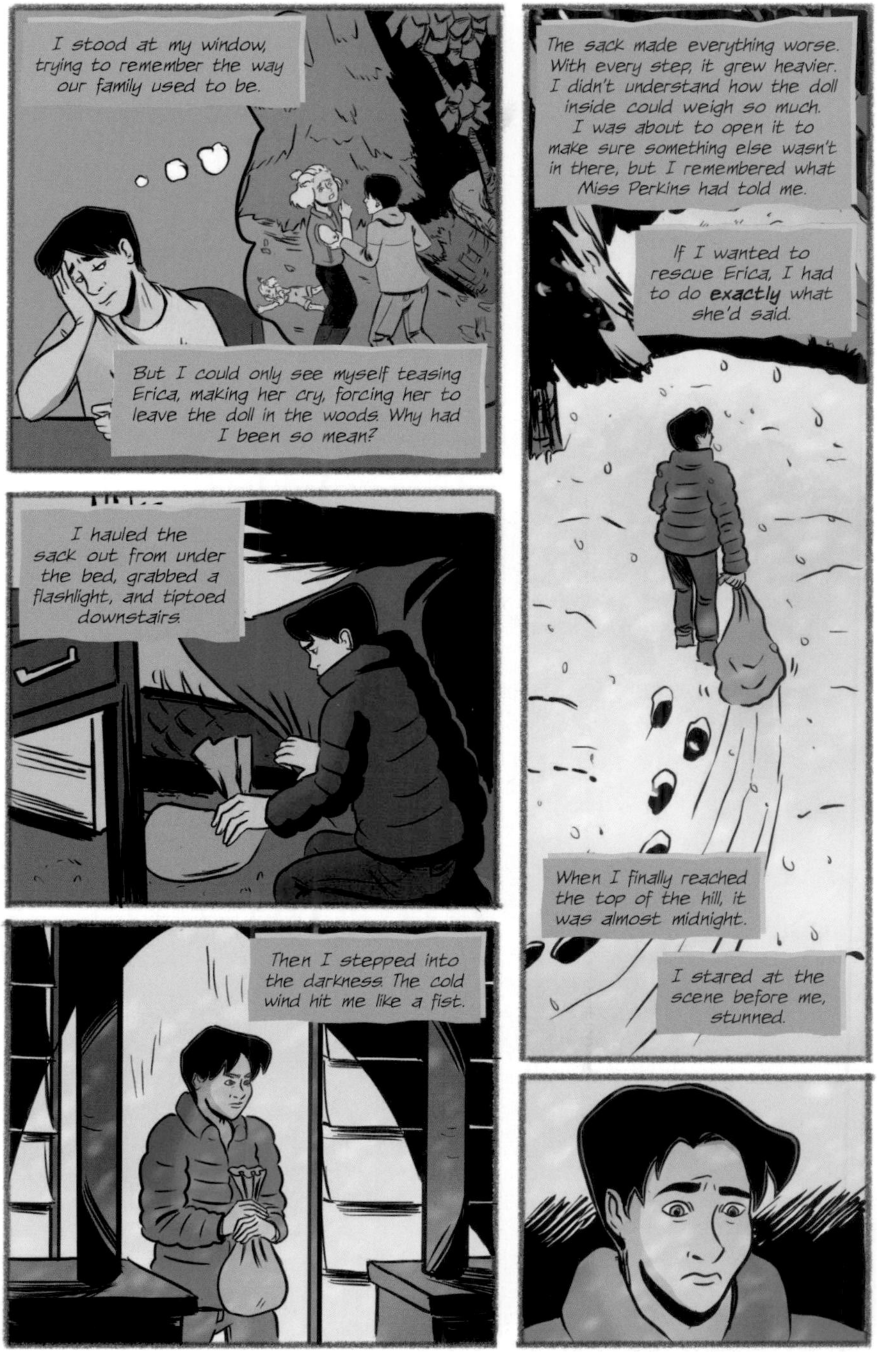
I stood at my window, trying to remember the way our family used to be.
But I could only see myself teasing Erica, making her cry, forcing her to leave the doll in the woods. Why had I been so mean?
I hauled the sack out from under the bed, grabbed a flashlight, and tiptoed downstairs.
Then I stepped into the darkness. The cold wind hit me like a fist.
The sack made everything worse. With every step, it grew heavier. I didn't understand how the doll inside could weigh so much. I was about to open it to make sure something else wasn't in there, but I remembered what Miss Perkins had told me.
If I wanted to rescue Erica, I had to do **exactly** what she'd said.
When I finally reached the top of the hill, it was almost midnight.
I stared at the scene before me, stunned.

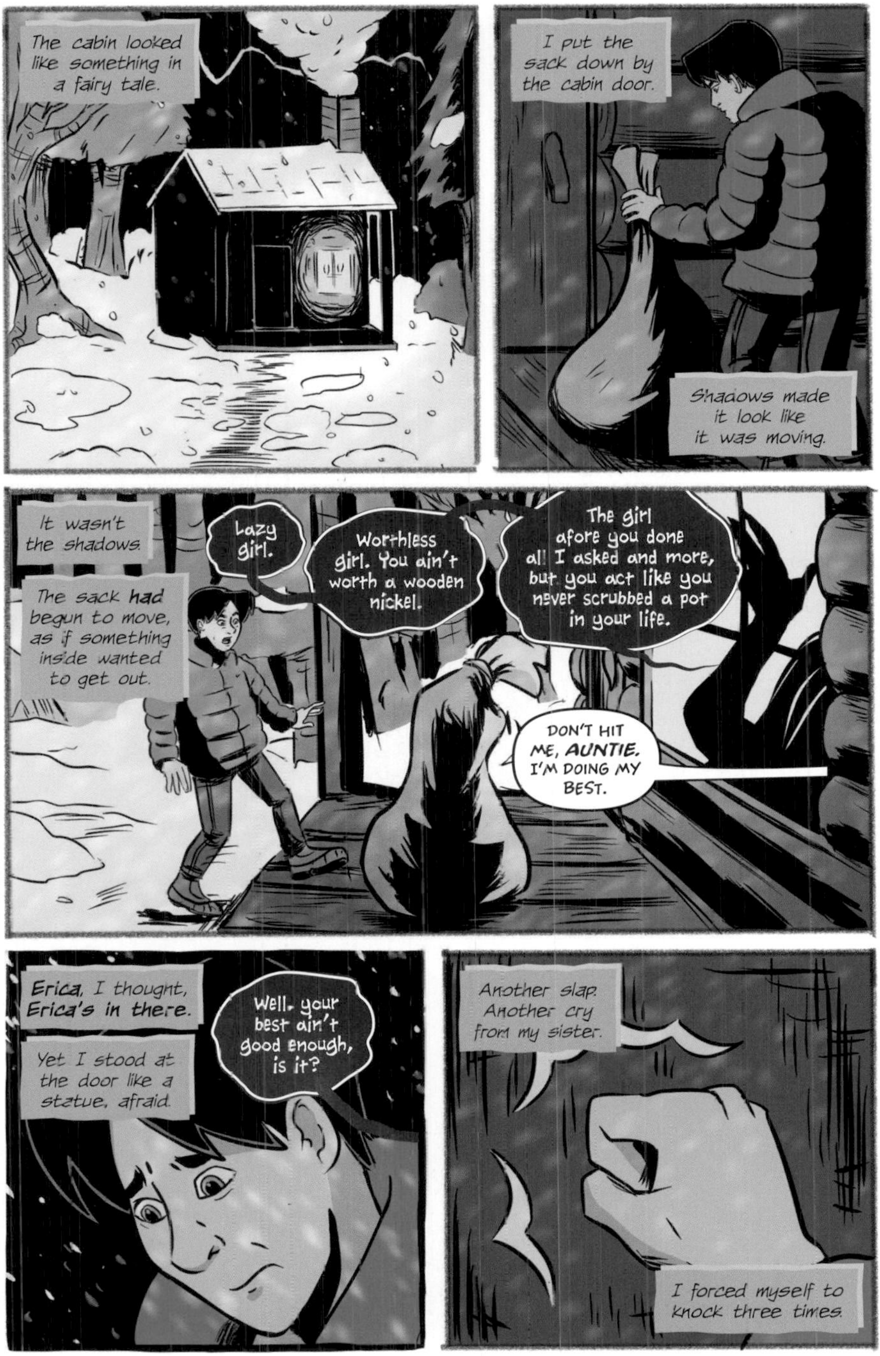
The cabin looked like something in a fairy tale.
I put the sack down by the cabin door.
Shadows made it look like it was moving.
It wasn't the shadows.
The sack **had** begun to move, as if something inside wanted to get out.
Lazy girl.
Worthless girl. You ain't worth a wooden nickel.
The girl afore you done all I asked and more, but you act like you never scrubbed a pot in your life.
DON'T HIT ME, **AUNTIE.** I'M DOING MY BEST.
Erica, I thought, **Erica's in there.**
Yet I stood at the door like a statue, afraid.
Well, your best ain't good enough, is it?
Another slap. Another cry from my sister.
I forced myself to knock three times.

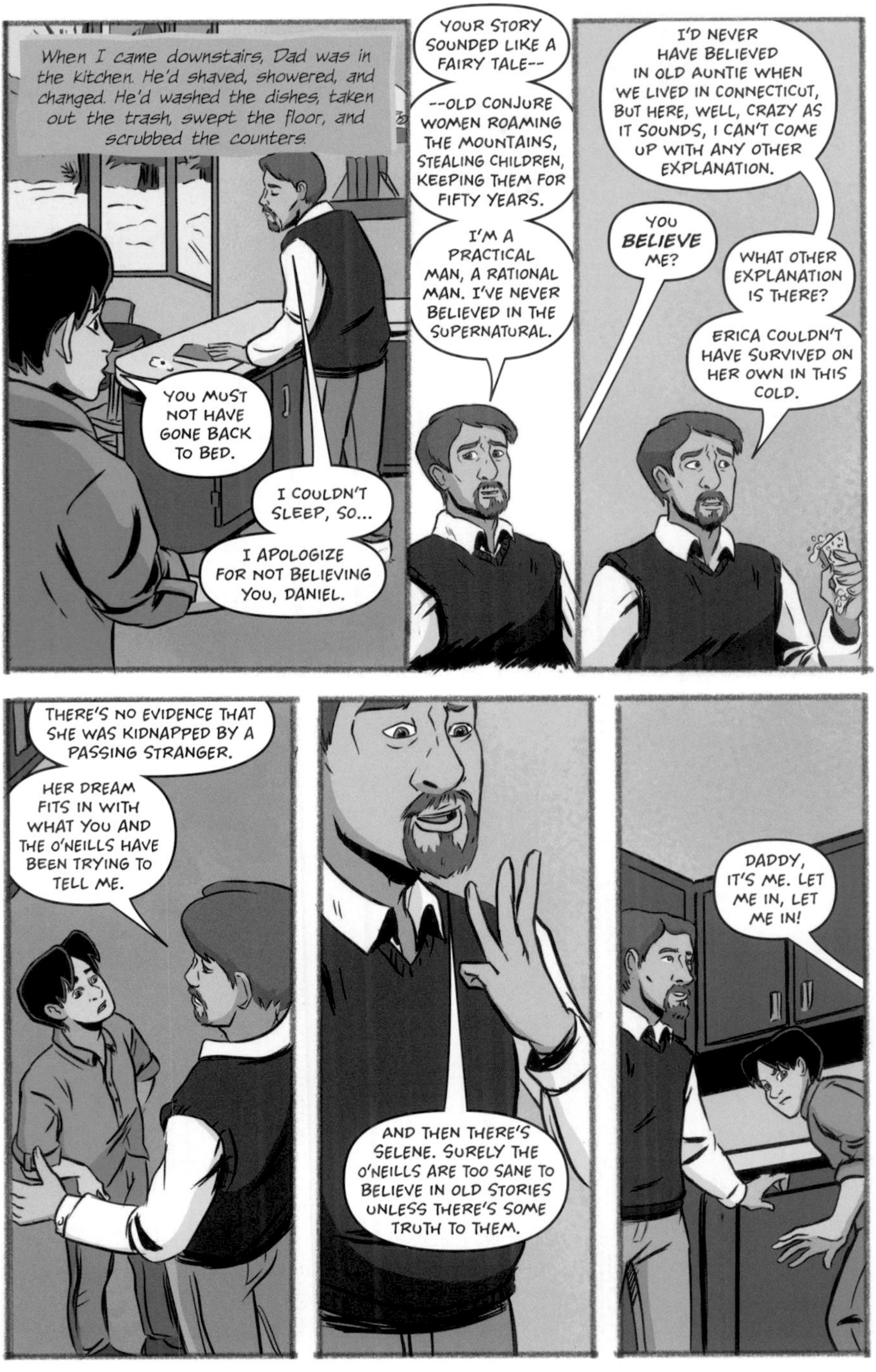
When I came downstairs, Dad was in the kitchen. He'd shaved, showered, and changed. He'd washed the dishes, taken out the trash, swept the floor, and scrubbed the counters.
YOU MUST NOT HAVE GONE BACK TO BED.
I COULDN'T SLEEP, SO...
I APOLOGIZE FOR NOT BELIEVING YOU, DANIEL.
YOUR STORY SOUNDED LIKE A FAIRY TALE--
--OLD CONJURE WOMEN ROAMING THE MOUNTAINS, STEALING CHILDREN, KEEPING THEM FOR FIFTY YEARS.
I'M A PRACTICAL MAN, A RATIONAL MAN. I'VE NEVER BELIEVED IN THE SUPERNATURAL.
I'D NEVER HAVE BELIEVED IN OLD AUNTIE WHEN WE LIVED IN CONNECTICUT, BUT HERE, WELL, CRAZY AS IT SOUNDS, I CAN'T COME UP WITH ANY OTHER EXPLANATION.
YOU **BELIEVE** ME?
WHAT OTHER EXPLANATION IS THERE?
ERICA COULDN'T HAVE SURVIVED ON HER OWN IN THIS COLD.
THERE'S NO EVIDENCE THAT SHE WAS KIDNAPPED BY A PASSING STRANGER.
HER DREAM FITS IN WITH WHAT YOU AND THE O'NEILLS HAVE BEEN TRYING TO TELL ME.
AND THEN THERE'S SELENE. SURELY THE O'NEILLS ARE TOO SANE TO BELIEVE IN OLD STORIES UNLESS THERE'S SOME TRUTH TO THEM.
DADDY, IT'S ME. LET ME IN, LET ME IN!

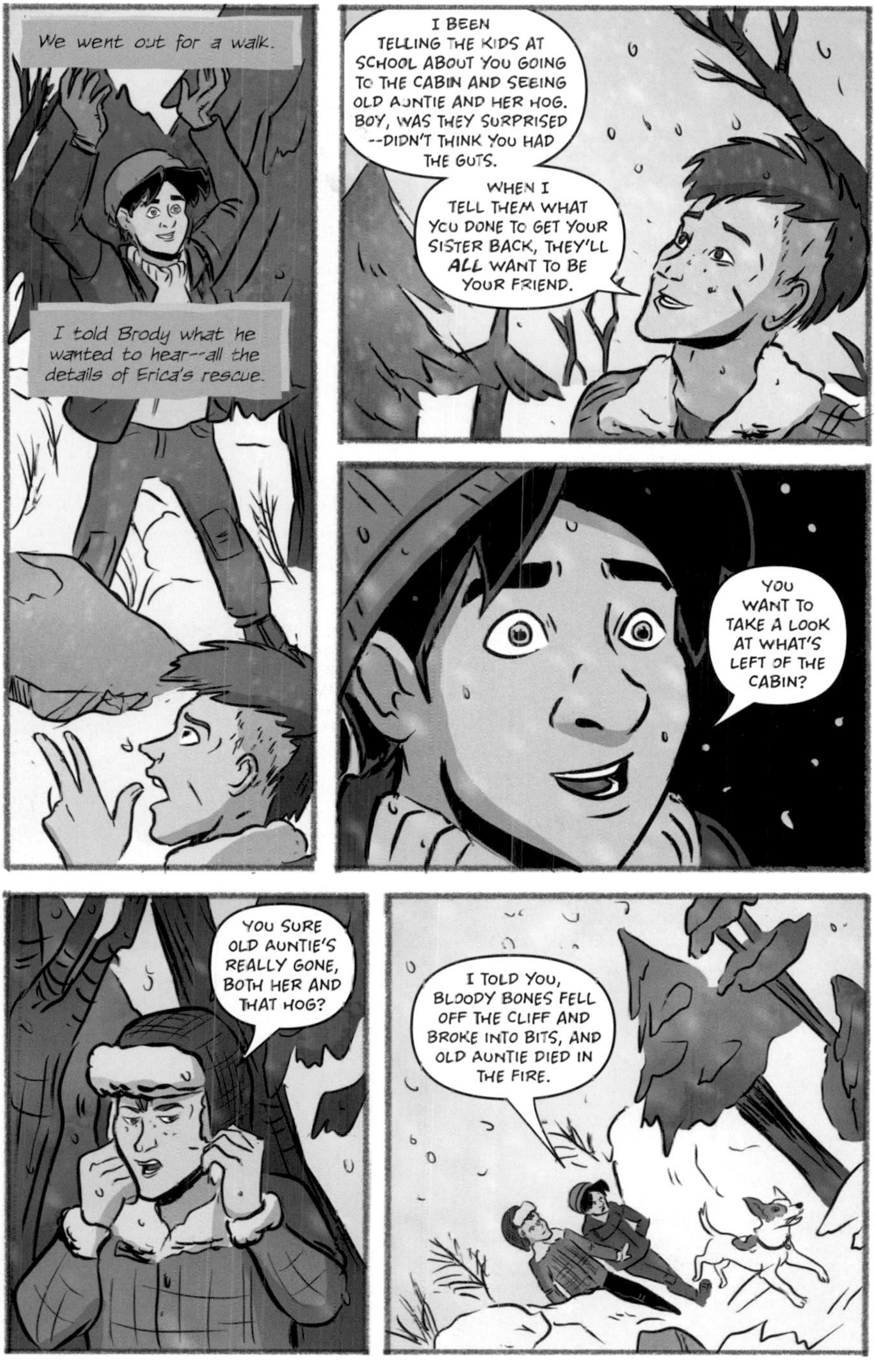
We went out for a walk.
I told Brody what he wanted to hear--all the details of Erica's rescue.
I BEEN TELLING THE KIDS AT SCHOOL ABOUT YOU GOING TO THE CABIN AND SEEING OLD AUNTIE AND HER HOG. BOY, WAS THEY SURPRISED --DIDN'T THINK YOU HAD THE GUTS.
WHEN I TELL THEM WHAT YOU DONE TO GET YOUR SISTER BACK, THEY'LL ALL WANT TO BE YOUR FRIEND.
YOU WANT TO TAKE A LOOK AT WHAT'S LEFT OF THE CABIN?
YOU SURE OLD AUNTIE'S REALLY GONE, BOTH HER AND THAT HOG?
I TOLD YOU, BLOODY BONES FELL OFF THE CLIFF AND BROKE INTO BITS, AND OLD AUNTIE DIED IN THE FIRE.

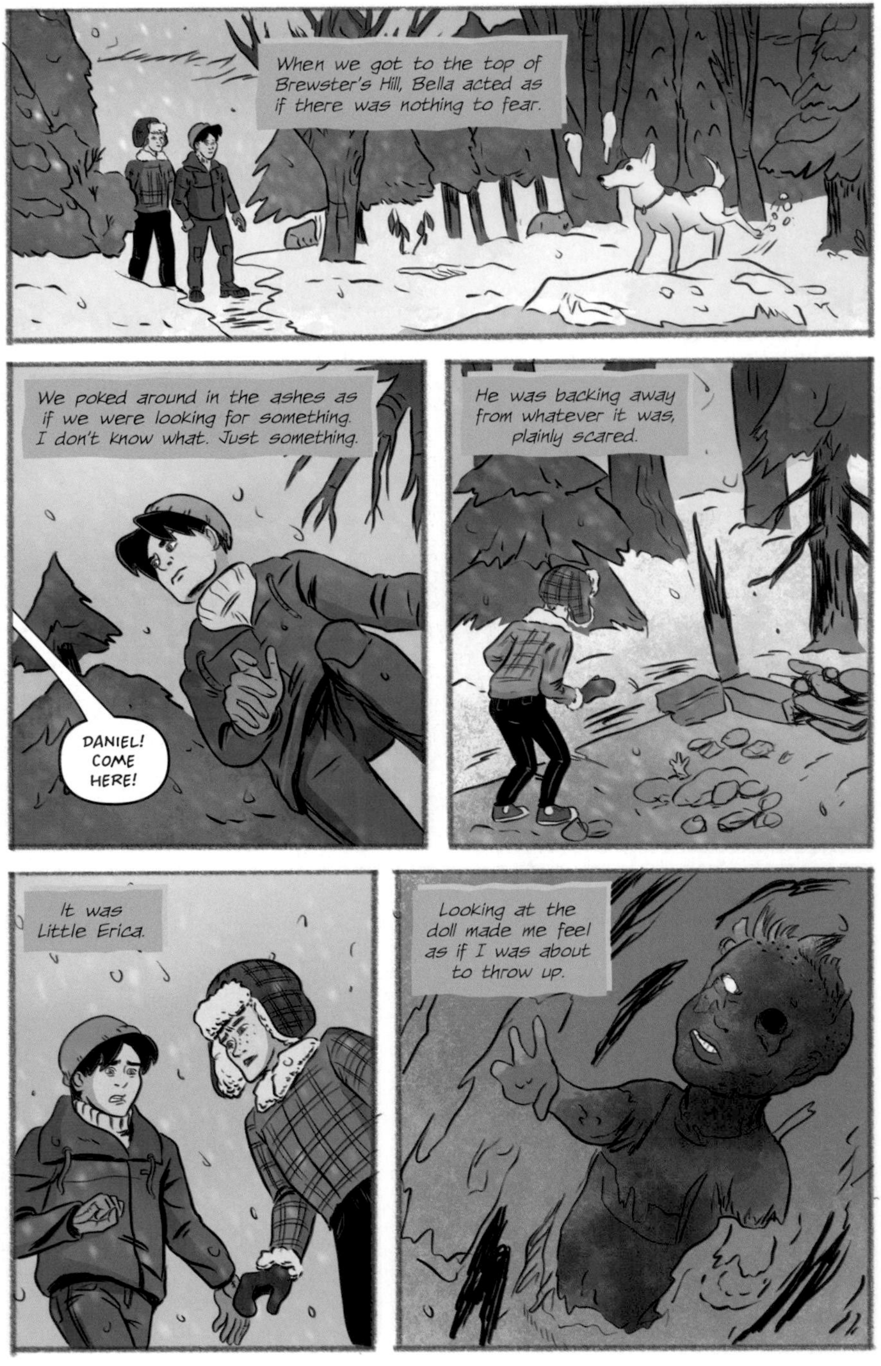
When we got to the top of Brewster's Hill, Bella acted as if there was nothing to fear.
We poked around in the ashes as if we were looking for something. I don't know what. Just something.
DANIEL! COME HERE!
He was backing away from whatever it was, plainly scared.
It was Little Erica.
Looking at the doll made me feel as if I was about to throw up.